The Boy Who Rode The Rails

Brent S. Furrow

Table of Contents

Copyright   2
Chapter 1   5
Chapter 2   8
Chapter 3   12
Chapter 4   16
Chapter 5   21
Chapter 6   25
Chapter 7   28
Chapter 8   32
Chapter 9   38
Chapter 10   43
Chapter 11   49
Chapter 12   52
Chapter 13   57
Chapter 14   61
Chapter 15   70
Chapter 16   79
Chapter 17   82
Chapter 18   86
Chapter 19   90
Chapter 20   93
Chapter 21   99
Chapter 22   103
Chapter 23   106
Chapter 24   112
Chapter 25   122
Chapter 26   125
Chapter 27   128
Chapter 28   133
Chapter 29   139
Chapter 30   143
Chapter 31   147
Chapter 32   151
Chapter 33   155
Chapter 34   160
Chapter 35   163
Chapter 36   168

Chapter 37   173
Chapter 38   180
Chapter 39   183
Chapter 40   187
A Note From The Author   191

Copyright

The Boy Who Rode The Rails
Copyright © 2025 Brent S. Furrow
(Defiance Press & Publishing, LLC)

Published by Defiance Press & Publishing, LLC
Bulk orders of this book may be obtained by contacting Defiance Press & Publishing, LLC. www.defiancepress.com.
Defiance Press & Publishing, LLC
281-581-9300
info@defiancepress.com

Dedicated to those who
presently live an adventurous youth,
Those who longingly
recount adventures from their youth,
Those who truly believe in young love,
And those who recognize that God is present in all.

Chapter 1

There is surely a future hope for you, and your hope will not be cut off.
Proverbs 23:18 (NIV)

In my younger years, my mother often quoted my father's proverbial wisdom: "Whenever you feel like criticizing anyone, just remember that all the people in this world haven't had the advantages that you've had." It was a poignant line, and one that I later learned that he borrowed from *The Great Gatsby*, a novel that resonated deeply with him—a line that would go on to have personal implications within the incredible and dynamic story of my youth.

I grew up in the impoverished town of Paxton, Alabama, during the 1950s and early 1960s, a working-class southern community heavily reliant upon the railroad and coal industries. The kind of place where a childhood is largely shaped by a town's economic struggles, and given my circumstances, my advantages and opportunities seemed limited at best. Sadly, I never had the chance to meet my father in person, nor absorb the firsthand wisdom he would impart. Although, as I would later learn, he would speak to me in the most peculiar way from beyond the grave.

I cannot tell the coming-of-age story of my life, of young love and heartbreak, hardship and prosperity, courage and timidity, and the great trajectory that would pivot my life beyond my wildest dreams without first conveying the mise-en-scène of which I grew up. The story of my youth begins with my mother who single-handedly raised me and the father whom I never had the chance to know—until a twist of events late into my teenage years would connect us through time and space far beyond the grave.

My father was drafted into the Second World War deep into the throes of its third year. No one thought that the "war to end all wars" would stretch that long, but late in 1943, as death took its ceaseless toll on young Americans fighting to preserve freedom and peace, the Marines soon joined the Army and Navy in drafting young men to fill its ranks. It was at this time that the War Department came knocking, and my father dutifully answered the call to join the United States Marines.

Before he was drafted, my father worked as the railroad stationmaster in Paxton, which handled a small amount of mail and passenger traffic that would come through the depot every day. Mostly, though, he managed the coal loading operations that fed the electric plants up north, along with bales of cotton laden onto boxcars, a vital economic lifeline for our little town.

My mother recalled to me that my father suspended his civilian railroad career and was ordered to report almost immediately for training. He completed boot camp in California before quickly shipping out to the South Pacific, where he landed on Kwajalein Atoll on January 31, 1944. It was on this desolate island half a world away where my father died instantly during his inaugural wartime mission, when a Marine demolition team unintentionally threw a cluster of high explosives into a Japanese bunker, not realizing that it was actually a torpedo warhead magazine.

Newspaper articles and newsreels recalled that when the tragedy took place, the explosion was so great it appeared as if the whole coral island blew right off the map; a great cloud of gunpowder and smoke that sent vibration ripples across the sea that even shuddered U. S. naval ships as they lay just offshore in berth. In a bittersweet consolation—if there is any such thing in war—at least he didn't suffer. No POW camp. No painful hospital stay. No Bhutan death march, or starvation or sickness while languishing in Nagoya or Sendai. Just a life gone in an instant, along with 20 other brave young men committed to the cause of suppressing the evil tyranny that was seemingly encapsulating the world in those days—a puff of smoke in the middle of the Pacific, as distant and removed from Alabama and the rest of the United States as you could possibly get.

Chapter 2

Prior to the war, the railroad provided our family with a modest stationmaster home in which to live, painted drab green but surprisingly ornately adorned with trusses and elaborate corbels in its construction several decades earlier, a nod to the prosperity of the Roaring Twenties. The main passenger depot in town sat adjacent to our home, which consisted of a small waiting lounge with a platform that existed as a minor whistle-stop in the midst of a network of southeastern railroads. The railroad line ran perpendicular to Main Street in town and created a T-intersection of sorts, with our house and depot situated just above the north parallel highway where Main Street ended.

A couple of years before my father was drafted into the Marines, the steam-powered trains that once ran regularly through our town had already been in steady decline, decreasing to but a trickle of their once-common frequency. Most of the railroads in the country were well on their way to converting to diesel engines, and during this period of technological advancement, the Alabama & Tennessee Railroad built a new line from Atlanta to Huntsville that could carry heavier loads, bypassing Paxton by some forty miles. When the regional coal mining operations crested at their peak, coinciding with the beginning of the decade-long dust bowl that dampened the cotton harvest, our town entered into a depression along with the rest of the country in the 1930s—of which it never would fully recover. This new heavy rail line carried most of the freight traffic that shunned our little town, which was largely forgotten. By the mid-1940s, even the interstate passengers opted for the Trailways bus system on a vastly improved highway network that was a direct result of the Works Project Administration's extensive road paving efforts of the late 1930s that vastly improved automobile travel.

My mother was three months pregnant with me when my father was drafted. She often recalled that she and my father exchanged love letters throughout his training, and from his first night in boot camp, he told her that his only objective in life was to return home to her. As high school sweethearts, they fell madly in love, and their affection remained steadfast and unwavering for as long as they were together. I envied that kind of relationship and hoped that someday I would be so fortunate to find that same kind of lifelong, unfaltering love and devotion with a spouse. Sadly, their love would be cut short, though. My mother was seven months pregnant with me when my father was killed in the war, and the final love letter that he drafted to her was poignantly received nearly a month after his body had returned home for final resting.

They say that when she received word of my father's death, my mother was in the middle of her shift as a waitress in the Redbird Cafe in Paxton. Two sharply dressed Navy sailors came into the cafe— the place of her first part-time job when she was in high school, and the only location of employment that she worked her entire life. The sailors asked her if she could step outside to speak to them, but the sight alone of them solidified her deepest fear that the news they were poised to relay was of imposing tragedy.

Years later, I was told that she went into sobbing hysterics in the middle of the diner and dropped to the floor in a moment of utter inconsolable mourning, where she blacked out. The patrons who were present and saw her body hit the floor that morning feared she would miscarry, and the busboy dashed across the street to the clinic to summon the town doctor to her aid. Her worst fear had come true, and as a couple whose identity was so mutually a part of each other, so tightly wrapped up in unity and solidarity, her grief in his loss was all too much to bear.

The day my father's remains were returned home for burial ironically coincided with the last steam train to ever pass through our little town. In a poignant twist of fate that this southern town, forged by the labor of its blue-collar men in the coal mines, saw its steam-powered railroad era come to an end on the very day that its chief stationmaster returned home in a flag-draped casket, carried by that final train. The mining decline in coal tonnage, along with diminished post-depression cotton harvests, irrevocably diminished the railroad's vitality. Paxton's vibrant legacy, born from the industry's initial reliance on rail transport, could no longer be sustained. As a result, the town's railroad operations were forced to shutter operations permanently.

War breaks up a man's life in a way unlike almost any other event in life. It is an opportunist counterfeit trade, one that shapes a man's destiny at the exact time that he should be starting his career as a machinist, a lawyer, a farmer—or, in the case of my father, a railroad stationmaster. There's an unspoken cruelty in how the beckoning of battle places certain demands upon a young man's life, and it becomes foreign afterward to reintegrate into a career at a factory or bank or office building after a daily routine of reveille and taps, marching and drills, and beans and bullets. And perhaps the detesting loss of a limb or faculty, or even fate itself, as war has the power to cut short not only the life of the soldier or sailor but also that of a young bride or children whose lives have been surreptitiously upended as casualties themselves.

Still more are those veterans whose personalities are a shadow of their former selves, a fading echo caught somewhere in the realm between depression and angst, anguish and night terrors, unable to fully assimilate back into their former culture and previously established interpersonal relationships. Their physical bodies may have surreptitiously escaped battles unscathed, yet the torture and anguish haunt on until one day the Lord decides they have suffered enough on this earth and calls them home.

Chapter 3

The afternoon train that arrived into the Paxton station carrying my father's funerary casket was adorned with red, white, and blue bunting flanking its sides. The town had organized a supportive gathering and patriotic memorial procession that would follow the transfer of my father's remains from the station to the church, only a few blocks away. Following the funeral, my pregnant mother, with me yet to be born, Charles, and his wife continued to the town cemetery for a private interment.

One of the senior railroad executives from Nashville who came to town for my father's funeral took pity on my mother, who by now was only a few weeks away from giving birth to me. He kindly gave her permission to continue living in the stationmaster's house since the Paxton station was mothballed due to the new rail line that was built. As long as my mother paid the utilities and kept the place up, the gentleman's agreement was that the home was ours until they found another use for it or there was some future need to reactivate the Paxton line. That blessing, while earnestly indispensable for my mother at the time, would foreshadow events to come that would change the trajectory of my own life—a boy yet to be born.

Along with the passenger station, the Alabama & Tennessee Railroad also maintained a rail car repair shop that sat a few hundred yards from our house. The tall, red-brick building, a relic of a forgotten age decades prior, stood sentinel against the encroaching wilderness beyond.

Overgrown helix ivy, a vibrant emerald green contrasting against weathered red brick, cascaded down its walls, creating an eerie, otherworldly beauty for as long as I could remember. Two sets of spur rails, abandoned and overgrown with kudzu and fireweed, led from the main track towards the building, directing passersby a glimpse into the town's past that had long since faded away. When the railroad closed the Paxton station, they closed the rail car repair operations as well. Men who worked there were transferred to other facilities in Nashville, Atlanta, and elsewhere throughout the system. As long as I had ever known it, the building and repair yard had sat in a state of decay as nature slowly reclaimed its place.

My brother Charles was eight years older than me. After his birth, the doctor, for reasons unbeknownst to me, informed my parents that my mother would unlikely be able to conceive again. Yet I was the unexpected surprise baby who came along years later. After my father's passing, my mother, a woman of incredible resilience, continued to work tirelessly at the Redbird Cafe. She juggled the demands of single parenthood, maintained our home, cultivated a modest garden to supplement her meager income from tips and wages at the cafe, and raised two boys in an era when life was particularly challenging for a widow.

Within a couple of years, my father's pension and measly life insurance from the Marines had begun to run low. Since money was tight, Charles went to work at the coal mine camp at age eleven. There he would empty trash cans, sweep floors in the superintendent's office and chow hall, and ensure water jugs for the men were topped off. He made twenty-five cents working each day after school for a few hours and a full dollar for a day's work on Saturday, all of which he would give to my mother to help keep food on our table and our kerosene lamps lit. The mine couldn't legally hire him as young as he was. But knowing my mother was a widow and being a kind and genuine friend of my later father, we later learned that the mine superintendent paid my brother's wages out of his own pocket in a repose of empathetic charity.

Life was tough, but we managed to survive and press onward. The post-war boom was a busy time for the rest of the country with great construction projects taking place in big cities all over the country, while in Paxton life seemed to evolve slower. Cotton crops eventually rebounded following the depression, and while the railroad line through Paxton never did restart, most of the cotton was trucked fifty miles or so over the vastly improved highway system to the Tennessee River, where the bales were then transferred onto barges to be sent to the mills.

The Alabama & Tennessee Railroad ended up going completely bankrupt a few years after the war ended, and the land where our home stood was seemingly forgotten in time. Mother lived in constant fear that they would evict us and send a bulldozer to demolish our home or that a new railroad would buy the spur line through Paxton, forcing us to move out at a moment's notice, but no one ever came. Our house, the old station, the large machine shop in the distance, a rust-brown water tower, and a few small miscellaneous outbuildings and scraps of old iron parts were the only remnants left from the steam railroad of yesteryear. My mother continued to pay the bills one way or another, and so long as creditors never came knocking to evict us, life trudged on.

Chapter 4

Twenty-four years old and now married, my brother had taken a post-high school job working as an apprentice in the hardware and feed store in town and later was promoted to become the manager of the entire enterprise. It was a decent-sized business, and farmers would come from all over to buy their seed for crop planting, tools, pesticides, and other implements and supplies needed for daily farm and home life. My favorite time to drop in to the store was during the springtime when they sold baby chicks, ducks, rabbits, and quail, and it was great fun to hold the soft balls of fluff in my hands. Mother continued working long hours at the diner, and although she and Charles never spoke of it to me, I suspected he would help her out with a little money from time to time to help make our ends meet.

My junior year of high school in 1961 was when everything began to change. School for me was a peculiar place, as I never fit in the way that all of the other students seemed to. I was known as a geek around the school thanks to the nicknames given by Boone and Oliver, two incorrigible high school bullies, since I highly favored my history and science classes and my academic acumen far excelled most. Through most of my high school career, I remained aloof and reticent and kept to myself as a result.

Every school seems to have its ne'er-do-wells and hoodlums, and my school was no different. Boone and Oliver Tybalt were a couple of brothers who lived on a century-old cotton plantation a few miles west of town. Their attire often consisted of tattered blue jeans, riddled with holes at the knees, and worn-out leather work boots, a testament to their strained home life. The only shirts I ever saw them wear were undershirts so aged by dirt and sweat that they looked as though they doubled as automobile oil dipstick rags from all of the chores their daddy made them do every morning before heading into school.

The Tybalt brothers looked like they had been born fighting right out of the womb, with chiseled teeth, tan muscular arms, and greasy mopped hair. Both were football players on the high school's eight-man football team, and were as solid with muscle from throwing bales of cotton on their farm as they were overweight from lack of proper nutrition. While poor ourselves, we always found a way to scrape by, Lord willing. But with a mother whom it was rumored ran away because of abusive conditions by their father, the Tybalt brothers were even more indigent and destitute. It certainly didn't help their plight that their daddy drank heavily, and it wasn't uncommon to see one of them— or sometimes both—show up to school with a black eye or bruises all over their arms from his rough disdain.

By the 1960s, mechanized agriculture was almost ubiquitous, as tractor technology had become commonplace nearly everywhere in the U. S. However, whenever riding my bike west of town, I would often see those boys and their daddy driving a team of mules to trench furrows in the earth for planting cotton in the springtime or using mule power to pull a flatbed cotton wagon through the fields in the fall. As obstinate and tough as they were, with frequent run-ins with authority and the law, most folks overlooked them except on the occasional autumn football Friday nights should they help pull our high school team to victory. I usually avoided them myself whenever possible, finding their behavior abrasive and difficult to tolerate, but my Christian upbringing implored me to at least extend grace and a little amity whenever possible.

My high school teacher, Mr. Smith, was my favorite instructor all through school, and he taught both freshman and sophomore literature as well as junior and senior science and history. It wasn't uncommon to have the same teacher all four years or for multiple subjects in our small school, and Mr. Smith always took a shine to me for some reason. Maybe he saw potential in me, or maybe he just saw that I longed for escape from this two-bit, dead-end town. Even my house at the T-intersection beyond Main Street was evocative of the unpleasant truth that Paxton was the literal end of the road for most.

With my strong interest and aptitude in school, though, the adventures I learned from textbooks would carry me a million miles away from the plight of this dying agrarian and coal community. Mr. Smith and I often found ourselves discussing higher thoughts than most of the other students cared for. He seemed to take a liking to me, or maybe it was simply out of pity, since he was of similar age to my father and likely would have been when drafted, but due to bone spurs, his 4-F draft card allowed him to escape the revulsion of war.

All the while, I knew that in his younger years Mr. Smith had heard the stories of returning soldiers—many a great men, but shells of themselves after witnessing the evils of tyrants and global empires colliding across the vastness of the world. Wounded in both body and spirit. Some of those veterans around town spoke no words, but you could see the longing in their eyes for bucolic and pastoral days, the youth of yesteryear before they were left with the resultant horrors of a war they were unwittingly sent to fight.

Mr. Smith's kindness, for whatever reason, led him to generously take me under his wing, a gesture I deeply appreciated. Inspired by his mentorship, I felt a strong drive to excel and earn the admiration of this teacher I greatly esteemed and respected.

During my junior year of high school, I took on a paper route to earn some extra cash. I often finished my deliveries an hour or two before the school bell rang. Afterwards, I'd make breakfast at home, just as my mother was leaving for work at the cafe. Since it was still too early to head to school, I'd often bike down to the cafe, hoping she might slip me an extra doughnut or some bacon out the back door if she wasn't too busy right at the start of her shift.

On other days, I'd arrive at school early and often find Mr. Smith setting up his classroom or reviewing the day's lessons. We'd sometimes discuss astronomy, with him pointing out which planets would be currently visible in the night sky. He'd share fascinating tidbits, like how "heating and cooling degree days" influenced local farming. In return, I'd sometimes share an interesting fact from the history books I would often read for adventure and escape, such as a random fact regarding the Battle of Gettysburg, the Raid on Harpers Ferry, or how steamship travel on the Mississippi River revolutionized American commerce and accelerated westward expansion. Sometimes we'd discuss music and our favorite artists or new songs, from The Four Tops to The Mamas and the Papas, Elvis, and even Sammy Davis Jr., popping a record on the turntable he kept in the classroom as we waited for the school day to begin.

I think the mental escape of adventure, travel, and plans bigger than anything going on in sleepy Paxton helped to give both of us a morning boost that would energetically carry us into the school day, and it was fun to daydream with a teacher who took a liking to me and seemed to be on a similar mental plateau. Without a father to grow up with, Mr. Smith fulfilled that paternal need since I found it so easy to converse with him on a variety of subjects and current events, and he instilled encouragement in me to explore and express my interests and passions.

Chapter 5

It was Chaucer who said, "All good things must come to an end," and coal mining hauls in northeast Alabama began to sharply drop by the middle of the century. By the early 1960s, layoffs were commonplace since mine production was merely a fraction of its once historic hauls. We had heard a rumor that the mine company was transferring in a new superintendent to try and increase the coal mine production once again. The prior superintendent, the gentleman who had extended grace to my brother Charles in the form of a job and a little money when we most needed it years earlier, was retiring after a nearly fifty-year career. The buzz around town was that with a new superintendent, the mine might begin producing coal hauls rivaling the level before the war—without understanding that the ground only has so much coal in it, and once it's depleted, it's gone for good. The volume of a coal vein is only so much, and even a senior geologist couldn't squeeze any more out of the earth if the mineral didn't exist. Still, with our town's population at just under a thousand people, the buzz of a new mine superintendent and a new family moving in was all the gossip. Although I, myself, shrugged off most of the buzz.

It was nearly the third week of my junior year that I noticed a young lady, unlike any I had ever seen before. I was rounding the corner to the schoolhouse, opting to walk that morning instead of riding my bike since the roads were still damp from an overnight rain. The smell of petrichor and geosmin hung heavy in the early morning air. Humming the tune to Bobby Rydell's "I've Got Bonnie" on my lips and casually dragging a stick along the top of the white picket fence that formed the perimeter of the schoolyard to hear the "click, click, click" sound, I looked up and saw her beautiful blue gabardine décolleté dress flowing in the breeze and the cutest chestnut brown ponytail bob in the air as she bounded up the steps of the school. I may have only seen the profile of her face from a distance, but it was as if Brigitte Bardot or Sandra Dee had sprinted up those steps. *But who was she? Why had my heart jumped like that? I must find out who she is!* I thought to myself.

Taking a deep breath, I paused for a moment, tossing aside the stick of which I had quickly lost interest, and I continued walking into the building. A few moments later, as I was rounding the corner to my locker, I saw her again. This time my blue eyes locked onto her deep brown doe eyes, and I coyly smiled but quickly looked away as we passed each other, afraid of what to mutter in spite of my shy self. I felt a sense of disgrace at what a sophisticated and beautiful girl with beautiful clothes should think of a poor, lanky, nerdy kid from the other side of the literal tracks.

As I turned to watch her walk away, I once again noticed she had the beautiful slender frame of Ann Blyth, one that would make any young man swoon. The mystery girl slipped into Mr. Smith's classroom at the end of the hallway, which was where I was headed in a few moments myself. I couldn't believe we were in the same grade, much less the same classroom. For once, I felt the universe smile down on me, and a ray of sunshine stretched out its open hand of beauty and generosity to send me butterflies in my otherwise mundane and bleak existence.

As I walked into class and sat down at my desk just as the bell was ringing, Mr. Smith introduced the new girl to all of us. Samantha Jensen was her name, he said, and he announced that her father was the new mining superintendent. The details were all starting to make sense—now I see why she moved to Paxton. *Samantha*, I thought, *how lovely and beautiful a feminine name!* Even better was that Samantha was assigned a previously empty desk right in front of mine, a moment of providential fortuitousness. I'd so fortunately get to study how the morning sun-kissed light filtered through the classroom window to make her auburn hair shine, the shape of her shoulders, and the soft, delicate peach fuzz on her arms every time she raised her hand to answer a question. My initial feelings for this girl were unlike anything I'd ever experienced.

Her presence enthralled and mesmerized me, leaving me spellbound. This unforeseen moment of hopeless romanticism revived new life in me, as if Cupid had just stung me with an arrow, a newfound eagerness and excitement at the thought of possibility. My prayerful hope was to become acquainted with this captivatingly beautiful new girl.

That night at home, I was still on cloud nine and couldn't get the image of the new girl, Samantha, out of my head. My mother had invited Charles and his wife, Millie, along with their newborn baby, Cordelia, over for dinner. We were all sitting at the kitchen table discussing the news, current events, and happenings of the day while having some of my mother's delicious peach cobbler when Charles spoke up and said he wasn't a fan of the new mine superintendent. My ears perked up. "Gary Jensen" was his name, he said, a big hard-headed, recalcitrant, gruff Norwegian. Always haggling at the hardware store and demanding he knock ten cents off a length of rope or a nickel off a box of nails. Usually husky and coarse, he said that this man was cheaper than dirt and never in a pleasant mood. It sounded as though he lacked any sort of cordiality and courtesy.

Ugh. . . Why must I have a crush on the daughter of such a stern curmudgeon? I annoyingly wondered to myself. I suppose much of his sternness was from the pressure that the mining board placed on him to try and squeeze more coal out of a mountain that only had so many ounces to give—a lofty, impossible weight upon his shoulders. But as the evening continued, I pondered the notion of Samantha's father and his briskness and cantankerous demeanor for the rest of the evening.

Chapter 6

The next few days at school passed quickly, and I had become accustomed to crossing paths with Samantha. My shyness slowly subsided, and I began making small talk every chance I got. "Where did you move here from?" "How long was the drive?" "Do you like your new house?" "What's your favorite Southern fried food that you've had so far?" I would ask her, attempting about any small-talk question I could think of just to hear her voice in reply.

One day, she mentioned that she forgot her lunch, and I happily shared my chicken salad sandwich with her. I watched her quickly devour it in a ravaging and what some might describe as an unrefined way, as you would customarily expect from a young lady. But something about her spunky energy and her avid personality was enticing as I studied the fine details and mannerisms she embodied. Those elemental traits made me fall even more head-over-heels for her.

We were quickly growing closer as friends, and I subtly endeared the way she would crinkle her nose and squint her eyes when she smiled, the gentle freckles that God had expertly placed below each of her eyes, and the thin wisps of sandy roan hair that hung down in front of her ears, even when her hair was pulled back in her signature classic ponytail. The smallest of details charmed and delighted me in a way of which I had never perceived about any other young woman before, and whether in her presence or not, I would constantly dwell on the loveliness of Samantha.

Homecoming at our school was in mid-October, only a couple of weeks away. Thoughts of Samantha continuously occupied real estate and residency in my mind—not that I minded one bit though, of course. But I mused quite seriously and deliberately about how I could carefully propose a plan of asking Samantha to the homecoming dance. *Should I show up early to school and surprise her with flowers?* No, that seemed a bit bold, and besides, where would she put them during the school day? They'd be withered and dead from being stuffed into her locker by the time class let out at 3:00. *Should I slip a note into her locker,* I wondered? No, that just seemed to lack effort and seemed largely impersonal. *Should I just straight up confront her and ask her?* Boldness and assertiveness annoyingly clashed with my timid and conservative coy style, so unless I could catch her alone to ask her in private, for fear of rejection in front of my other classmates, I wasn't sure I possessed the confidence to go that route either.

Before the day was through, though, rumors began to swirl that Boone had asked Samantha to the homecoming dance. Rumors, which I later confirmed with heartbreaking truth, struck me like a Brutus dagger into my heart. The age-old classic tale of a good girl ending up with a bad boy was true yet again. She didn't even really know him—not that she knew me any better, I suppose. But Boone and Oliver ran around in the circle of football jocks, and in a small town in Alabama, the football field was the epicenter of enticement, energy, and excitement on southern autumn Friday nights. Despite any bad-boy rap sheet of petty crime and minor vandalism, if you were worth your salt on the football field at all, you could easily become a local celebrity. I surmised after watching him play football that she was drawn to his athleticism and accepted his advance. The cute new girl decided to pursue the biggest jock—more like jackass—and despite manure always caked to his boots and constantly smelling of brome grass, I supposed she had a fascination with him unlike any she would ever have with me.

I certainly didn't possess the rugged charm like that of a young Robert Mitchum to win Samantha's heart. Neither svelte nor blessed with leading-man charisma, the lyrics of that old Irving Berlin song came to mind as heart-wrenching truth: "What chance have I, an ordinary guy? What chance have I with love?"

Chapter 7

The next two weeks seemed to drag on. I didn't muster the courage to ask anyone else to the dance, as I lamented in self-pity that the girl who stole my heart was already committed to Boone. Since I wasn't sure what else to do on a Friday night other than sit at home and play worn-out records or watch *The Bell Telephone Hour* on television, I decided I might as well go stag. Hopefully, a few of my other friends would be there, and I could hang out with them and pass the time. At least there would be cake and punch, if nothing else, a small sweetness of consolation.

The night of the homecoming dance, I dressed up in a polyester suit, brown skinny tie, and penny loafers and walked into the gymnasium shortly after the dance had started. The lights were dimmed to project a romantic mood, and someone had hung a mirror ball from the gymnasium ceiling that cast twinkling white lights onto the walls and floor. Crepe paper streamers were tied from the basketball rims to the walls, and cut-out paper decorations of pumpkins, leaves, and other fall themes adorned the gym. The school student council had done a pretty nice job of decorating and setting the theme of the fall dance.

I said hello to a few friends and struck up a little small talk with some other guys from my class who also went stag, and most of us sat on the third row of bleachers that were pulled out, scanning the crowd and occasionally refilling our cups of punch or grabbing some baked goods to munch on as we passed the time. A small bandstand was set up on the stage, and two different crooners took turns belting out Ricky Nelson and Roy Orbison songs, among other popular tunes.

A few times, I glanced out to see where Samantha was, curious if she was actually having any fun with the big oaf whose advance she accepted. At one point, they danced my way, and Samantha looked over Boone's shoulder at me and quietly mouthed "hello." I politely smiled with a "hello" reply as I watched them awkwardly spin off into the distance, a high school linebacker with his greasy black Brylcreem and butch wax hair, and a slender petite maiden with her thick, wavy flowing locks of auburn and gold, all in one *Tasmanian Devil* cyclone of a pair. It was quite a maladroit scene, had not the crush of my high school life been with my nemesis, the ungainly sight would have been worth quite a laugh, I suppose.

Feeling a bit down, dejected, and despaired, I couldn't stand the sight of Boone and Samantha anymore, so I excused myself from hanging with the classmates I was sitting with and exited the soirée to go for a walk alone through the dark, empty halls of the school. I wasn't being fair to myself to get this hung up over one silly girl, but such are the longings of an adolescent boy who believes in his serendipitous mind that his first crush will become his last love. After all, I so seldom met anyone new here in this little backwoods town, and my near-term future prospects seemed dim at best. As I walked aimlessly, with no plan or agenda, I stopped for a bit to peer into the vitrina in the school lobby. It was adorned with ribbons, medals, and trophies, showcasing everything from FFA championships to state basketball tournaments and spelling bee accolades. Considering my father had also attended this high school, I scanned the awards inside the showcase to see if I could spot his name, though any awards bearing his name eluded me.

Walking to the far end of the hallway, I peered into Mr. Smith's room and could see the dim outline of the classroom. Moonlight glinted off the chalkboard as an American flag silhouetted on a small pole stretched out at a forty-five-degree angle above it. The room was locked, but I wiggled the handle fervently. Surprisingly, the door popped open, so I stepped inside.

In the darkness, except for a full moon that cast its surreal iridescence through the window, I walked among the rows of chairs and tables. It was eerie to be in what otherwise was, in daylight, a lively classroom with lots of noise and commotion. In the corner of the room sat a new telescope, the product of a grant our school had won from the State of Alabama. Mr. Smith had mentioned in class that his plan was to organize an evening telescope viewing for anyone who wanted to come after dark and look through it, but he hadn't gotten around to setting a date yet. So the telescope sat idly by in the classroom during the daytime, a fascinating optical device that intrigued me, and one I had never before personally used.

In the silence of the night, the homecoming band now barely discernible, I decided to point out the classroom window toward the moon. Fiddling with the knobs and dials, the blurry whitewashed image eventually came into focus. The craters of the moon instantly came alive through this crisp October night sky, a Swiss cheese spectacle the likes of which I had only ever before seen in picture books. Kennedy had given his ambitious moon speech earlier in the year, and I was in awe of the possibility of man stepping foot on the moon before the end of the decade—if such a scientific achievement were even possible. Still, though, the thought fascinated me. If man were ever able to travel that far someday, how lonely it must feel looking back at the Earth. Home appearing so close in the mind's eye, everything familiar appearing so real in the consciousness of memory, yet at the same time the moon so tremendously distant from the Earth.

Lamenting how this night seemed like an utter loss and waste of time, I prayed and cried out to God that He would somehow change my life and lift it above the mire in which I felt such hopelessness. Stuck in a dead-end town, the girl I admired seemed to show no interest in me, and graduation was but a year and a half away with no real plan to go into a particular line of work nor the financial means to attend college. I poured out my fears, sadness, and sorrow in a soft-spoken prayer.

Chapter 8

I must have fallen asleep because when I heard the hoot of an owl in a tree outside the window, I was jolted awake. My neck was killing me from the awkward angle in which I had been hunched over. I found myself still sitting in a chair while my head was using the cold radiator coils next to the telescope as a pillow. *Ouch,* I thought, as I stretched my neck from side to side.

As I stood up, I glanced at the analog clock that hung on the classroom wall above the flag, which read 12:15 a.m. Way after curfew, and hoping that my mother had long since fallen asleep and had forgotten about my absence, I figured I could probably sprint the twenty-five-minute walk home in under ten minutes, even in my dress loafers, and slip in the back door without her noticing. If she was awake, however, my name would probably be mud, and she'd be feckless with worry about where I was at such a late hour.

As I walked the school hallway back to the front door, my neck still stiff with pain from napping on the radiator, I peered into the gym. Everyone had long since gone home, and the scene was quiet. All of the lights were off except for the red glow of the exit signs at the far end, and through the shadows, I could see little else but tinsel and some crepe paper streamers that had fallen onto the floor. I truly was the only person left in this eerily empty and silent building, and since no one knew I had slipped into a darkened classroom for escape, no one knew to come looking for me or to chase me out after the dance ended.

In a peculiar and piercing thought, I pondered once again how, if someday man were to step foot on the moon, at least they would be able to instantly communicate with someone on Earth through radio transmissions or Morse code. Their loneliness thousands of miles away would be less than mine was in this darkened school building without another soul around, in a strange sort of way.

As I exited the school building to head home, carefully pulling the door closed behind me to re-lock it, a fine mist hung in the air. One beautiful elemental substance of fall nights in our part of northern Alabama is how amorphous terrestrial fog settles in the valley between hilltop ridges, the result of cool night air moving in over the warmer ground below. On evenings like this, when Mother Nature's recipe is perfectly orchestrated, evoking a fall spookiness and phantasmagoric setting that always makes me think of the misty nighttime tarmac scene in *Casablanca*.

In a brisk pace I began to power walk toward home. Almost halfway to my house, through the fog and the mist, I could see a wrecked pickup truck in the distance, its lights still on, the front end punctured by a large tree trunk. Worried that someone might be hurt, I quickly jogged up to the scene, and upon reaching the red truck, I could hear the hiss of the radiator that appeared to be creating steam, which blended into the thick foggy night air. The wreck must have happened just moments before I exited the school, as I hadn't heard the slam of the accident happen, which would have been quite audible on a night as still as this.

Condensation on the windows prevented me from identifying who might be in the cab, but as I opened the driver's side door to peer inside, there sat Boone—with Samantha next to him on the passenger side of the bench seat —both of them dazed and woozy and slumped over, but thankfully no major blood that I instantly noticed. My heart sank, *what in the world just happened?!* There was not another automobile or soul around, which was not uncommon this late at night in our small rural town. Had I not walked by at just that moment, they might not have been discovered until morning.

My Eagle Scout training immediately kicked in, and I quickly and carefully pulled Boone and Samantha out, both of whom were banged up pretty badly but thankfully only appeared to have superficial injuries. Both could at least partially stumble out on their own two feet, a thankful sign, since there was no way my tall but scrawny frame could have lifted Boone the least bit. The stench of grain alcohol was on each of their breaths, and I could tell that both were in a drunken state. The force of the crash must have knocked them both loopy.

As I put Samantha's arm behind my neck to help get her out of the truck and onto the ground and leaned her up against the rear tire, I heard her say to me, "Aww, you came to my rescue. You really do like me!"

In the moment, I was more concerned with ensuring that they were both safe from danger, and my adrenaline didn't permit me to fully process if she was actually speaking to me or if she was so groggy that she actually intended those endearing words for Boone. Never mind any sort of feelings, resentments, or longings I had in the moment, though. Still in rescue mode, I knew that I urgently needed to get help.

As I stood up, I told them both that I would be right back, though I'm not sure that either of them comprehended my words. Another block and a half toward Main Street, I remembered that there was a pay phone where I could call our town police officer, Sheriff Johnson. Sprinting over to the phone booth and reaching for ten cents in my pocket to dial his home phone, I knew that nobody would be at the police station after hours. His home line was one of the dozen or so numbers my mother made my brother and I commit to memory in case there was ever an emergency. The sheriff groggily answered, since I clearly woke him up at such a late hour but said he would be right over. I then sprinted back to the scene of the wreck to check on my two classmates.

By this time, both had passed out and fallen over from where I had leaned them up against the truck's two opposite rear tires. They were asleep in the grass, still in their dance clothes and now dirty from the late-night dew and damp ground. There wasn't much else I could do, so I waited until the sheriff arrived. When Sheriff Johnson's patrol car pulled up with its single red beacon on top cutting through the foggy night air, both Boone and Samantha quickly awoke and sobered up.

After some intense questioning, Boone admitted that after the dance, he and Samantha went back to his plantation shanty for a bonfire where he, his brother, and his dad lived. By the time Boone and Samantha arrived there, he said that his father was already three sheets to the wind from drinking moonshine pretty heavily all evening long. His daddy had since gone inside their shanty and passed out for the night, but Boone stoked the embers and threw a few more logs on the bonfire to rebuild it, and he and Samantha got to drinking the leftover moonshine pretty heavily.

Moonshine was always a part of rural southern life in those days, and even during Prohibition, the old-timers said that you could always get your hands on some of the devil's juice. Since Prohibition ended, moonshine wasn't bootlegged nearly as heavily. But since distilling and selling it wasn't regulated by the state; the activity was still outlawed. That didn't mean that it still couldn't be found pretty easily, though.

As Boone confessed to the sheriff, after the two had been drinking for an hour or so, he got the wise idea to go for a drive with Samantha over to the city reservoir to skip stones—which, reading between the lines, I took to mean likely necking and skinny dipping, since who can see stones skip across water on a foggy night—but they never even reached the other side of town before crashing in his inebriated state.

Sheriff Johnson nodded in agitated disgust from being called out of bed in the middle of the night for such a dumb accident with the town's notorious ruffian, but I could tell he was relieved that there were no major personal injuries to either one, which likely meant less midnight paperwork. He reached inside Boone's truck and turned off the Ford 100's headlights, taking the keys out of the ignition and putting them in his own pocket. After that, he told the two to hop in the back of his patrol car, and he would take them both home. I said goodnight to the sheriff and continued my walk back to my house as they drove off.

In those days, the wrath of an embarrassed parent would be ten times worse than the slap on the wrist and menial fine a kid might get. I knew Boone's dad to be a degenerate drunk himself, so I doubted much would come of the situation to enact any real change with Boone. Probably a thick beating still for wrecking his pickup, though, no doubt. But I was more concerned about Samantha since she was small and delicate, and I knew her dad had a reputation for being gruff and stern and commanding a tight ship.

As I reached home and walked through the back door, my mother had in fact gone to sleep as I had hoped, and I avoided the particular squeaky floorboards that I knew from experience would creak as I climbed the stairs for my bed. I lay awake for a while, unable to sleep as I came down from my adrenaline rush from stumbling onto the accident. Staring at the ceiling, I wondered what kind of punishment Samantha was getting right about now—both for drinking and for likely breaking her curfew. It would be a long rest of the weekend before I'd get to see her at school again.

Chapter 9

Monday morning in class, our history lesson consisted of Paxton's role in the Civil War, a topic which I was excited to learn. Mid-morning and well after the start of the school day, Samantha came walking in with her head pretty bruised and a bandage on her chin from the car crash. I figured that her father probably wanted to run her to the town clinic to be checked out once it opened, so that explained her tardiness. Word travels fast in small communities and keeping a personal event like that a private secret was never truly a possibility.

The entire class let out an "Ooooh!" as she stepped into the classroom, and she paused for a second, glancing at Mr. Smith—and then directly at me—before walking hastily to her seat. *Why did she glance at me?* That was strange. I sat motionless as only my eyes followed her back to her desk ahead of mine where she took her seat. Leaning forward then, I whispered, "I'm glad you're okay," as she settled into her seat—loud enough that I wanted her to hear, but quiet enough that I hoped she wouldn't turn around in the midst of the already embarrassing moment.

Following the short pause, Mr. Smith pressed forward in his lesson of the day, and asked if anyone knew of our town's role in the Civil War. Oliver raised his hand and said that he knew that where his daddy, Boone, and he lived had once been part of a larger cotton plantation. It was built just a couple of years before the Civil War broke out and was called the Turnball Plantation. When the Union forces invaded the

South, he said that his father told him they burned the plantation home to the ground but left the slave quarters alone. John Turnball was away fighting for the Confederacy when Union forces set the mansion ablaze, and he was later killed in a small skirmish near Savannah, Georgia, when General Sherman of the Union army conducted his famous march to the sea. Turnball himself had previously sent his wife and four children back north to his in-laws' place in Worcester, Massachusetts, for their own safety when the situation looked imminent that the Union would invade North Alabama.

Oliver continued on and said that his daddy told him that when he built their two-room shanty, he repurposed a bunch of the original timbers from the last of the old slave cabins that still dotted the property, albeit in extremely decrepit shape. Then Boone, still black and blue in the face from wrecking his truck, raised his hand and said that he and Oliver were digging in the dirt near the old Turnball Mansion's foundation when they were younger and found a couple of old coins and some silver cutlery.

For a couple of hillbilly kids, they actually seemed to know a bunch of interesting history with which I was unfamiliar. Over the years, I have become somewhat acquainted with the legend of the Turnball Plantation, but not some of the other details that Oliver mentioned. My wonder was piqued if there could be other relics hidden within the dirt foundation of the old mansion—which by now, in the 1960s, had large saplings growing up inside the middle of the rubble and what was left of its original foundation.

Mr. Smith then taught about the region's railroad history and its importance in the Civil War and asked if anyone had ever heard the legend of the *Tullahoma?* Nobody raised their hand, but Mr. Smith said that's where we would pick up tomorrow.

As I sat there half daydreaming and in a daze as I observed the sunlight glinting off Samantha's smooth hair, with a cute bow she had chosen for today. The elements of her beauty contrasted with the bruises and scratches on her face from the wreck. I felt so dumb for ever having a crush on someone who would offer unrequited love in return. Friends were probably all we would ever be, and I supposed that despite the crash, she would likely still find a way to return to Boone.

Nice girls always fall hard for bad boys, they say—a tale as old as time, and one that I had begun to accept as a true cosmic reality—even if her daddy had forbidden her to ever see him again, which I assumed by now he had. They'd probably just be sneakier about their carousing. *Maybe she really wasn't the girl for me after all, if that's all the better her judgment is?* I proudly thought to myself in a mental sense of annoyance. But then the greater, more honorable Christian in me instantly regretted that I should have such self-righteous arrogance and trivialize her character simply because of a poor moment of lapse in judgment. We've all done and said regrettable things I thought to myself and I then felt a bit of self-shame.

As Mr. Smith was wrapping up for the class and everyone was beginning to stir as they gathered their belongings, without turning around Samantha slyly reached a hand back behind herself toward me down low. I was caught off guard, but in her hand folded up, I could see a note. As I took it from her, my fingers paused just a quarter of a second longer than they needed to in order to momentarily touch her warm, soft fingers as I took the paper from her grasp. My throat suddenly got a lump.

I hesitated to open the piece of paper as my mind raced to brace myself for what the note might say. Despite my mental catastrophizing, I was still besotted with love—as love in a young man's heart has a shrewd way of keeping hope alive.

Why would she be passing me a note? Well, I did save her life two nights before, so maybe it was just a thank you? No way, it wasn't like her life was actually in danger. More like a fender bender, and I'm making it out to be as if it were some huge life-and-death event. Well, I suppose it could have been life and death if the engine would have blown up. But do automobile engines actually blow up, or is that only something that happens in the movies? Well, didn't James Dean's car blow up when he crashed? I can't remember for sure. But forget James Dean—if Samantha and Boone had made it to the reservoir and she would have drowned because she was intoxicated, that could have been fatal. Or she could have been bitten by a snake; after all, you don't swim in a lake after dark in Northern Alabama in October when the copperheads come out. On cool nights, they're pretty active as they move around and look for a warm place to bed down for the winter though. Good gosh. By then, my mind was running off the rails, and I finally convinced myself to just open the darn thing.

As I walked out of the classroom toward my locker and unfolded the note, it wasn't actually a note from Samantha at all, but rather from her father, Mr. Jensen. The piece of paper said that he wanted to meet with me, that he'd be taking off work early from the coal mine later today and asked if I would please meet him in front of the Redbird Cafe at 3:30 after school.

My chest suddenly tensed again, and I got a lump in my throat. *Gulp!* I knew that he was a hard man, but I had no idea why he wanted to meet me. I didn't think I had done anything wrong. True, I had sneaked into the science room where I shouldn't have been during the dance, and I was still in the building after the dance ended. But that's not of concern to him. Plus, nobody besides me even knew I was there, and I hadn't actually hurt anything, so that couldn't be it. Besides, I had simply unintentionally fallen asleep, and I never had any ill intent to steal or damage anything. Maybe he was angry that I involved the law after the accident and would've rather I just stayed out of it—left things for him to handle strictly as a family matter himself? But in my defense, at that time I had no way of knowing if Samantha or Boone were actually hurt, so I thought that going to get help was the best decision in the moment. *It wasn't like I could have just left them there on the side of the road,* I thought.

There my mind goes, running on overdrive again. Time to man up, though, and just honor his request. If I completely ignore it, I would ruin ANY chance of gaining a single ounce of his respect. Plus, even if there was no chance of romance, I intently hoped that Samantha and I could at least maintain the cordial friendship we had built the past few weeks.

Chapter 10

The walk down to Main Street that afternoon after school was long. . . and a bit unnerving. As I impatiently waited on the curb in front of the diner, a gorgeous all-red Buick Skylark pulled up in front. A man stepped out and asked for me by name, and I said that it was I. He introduced himself as Mr. Gary Jensen, Samantha's father. I had never met him nor seen him before now, only through the stories that I had heard. He stood a solid six foot three and wore cowboy boots, brand-new dark blue Levi's, and a plaid button-down shirt. He appeared as an intimidating-looking working man, and I could picture how his Norwegian ancestors were probably fierce Vikings. He embodied a John Wayne sort of larger-than-life taciturnity without the need to even utter a word and epitomized the essence of respect and honor, which elicited the same in return. As he held out his giant right hand to shake mine, I tried my best to match the same bone-crushing grip of strength with which he grasped mine, his strong, grizzled hand reinforced by years of manual labor before achieving a mine superintendent management role.

My throat got an instant lump in it, and although the extension of a handshake seemed to indicate he came in peace, I was thankful I was standing on the public sidewalk within view of other bystanders should I have completely misread the situation.

"Thank you so much for coming to my daughter's aid on Friday night," he told me. He continued that things had been very stressful moving to a new town with his wife, Samantha, and her younger sister, Kathryn, and that Samantha got mixed up with a bad guy like Boone, to which he was pretty disappointed.

Well, that's not entirely untrue, I thought to myself, biting my tongue on all of the dirt I could have told him about Boone. But I let him continue. He told me that he had heard stories of my father from the men at the mine and other townsfolk he had met since moving here. When he heard that I, my father's son, was the one who had come to his daughter's rescue on Friday night, he knew I must be a decent and honorable guy and would be elated if I took good care of his daughter. He also said that although he wasn't much of a church-going guy, he had heard that I attended services every week and would be more than happy if I ever wanted to ask Samantha to go with me some Sunday. As he continued, Mr. Jensen said that Samantha would be grounded for a while, and her chore list to seek penitence for drinking and breaking curfew was a mile long, but church and school were essentially the only places she could leave their home for.

There was that lump in my throat again, and my eyes welled up a bit at the humble honor that Mr. Jensen extended to me with his blessing, and how wonderful it would be if Samantha ever wanted to hang out with me. But *Take good care of his daughter?* I thought. What exactly did that mean?

"What about Boone though?" I said.

"Son," he told me, "There is absolutely *no way* I am ever going to let my daughter go out with that degenerate again. You may not realize it," he told me, "but you're actually the *only* person Samantha ever talks about."

Really?! I thought to myself. No doubt, the mind of a woman is a complicated and often inscrutable thing, one that I have never been able to discern or figure out. I thought of Proverbs 25:2 that sums it up pretty well with, "It is the glory of God to conceal a matter; to search out a matter is the glory of kings," and He did a fantastic job of creating a woman's mind with a combination harder to crack than that on the vault in Fort Knox. In my young life, I quite often misjudged what girls thought of me and never seemed to get it right, missing all the signs. However, the challenge for any young man to decipher the complexities of the female mind and what they are thinking is an all-consuming and intriguing pursuit, akin to uncovering the mystery of God Himself.

He went on, "She told me that she noticed you on her very first day at her new school while she was walking down the hallway. She actually wanted to go to the homecoming dance with you, but Boone just happened to ask her first. And not knowing if you would ask her out in time, she reluctantly accepted his invitation so she'd at least have *someone* to go with."

It WAS me all along, I thought, giving myself a boost of confidence that I had needed for so badly.

In a Proustian moment, I hearkened back to the accident scene when Samantha told me, "Aww, you really do like me. You came to my rescue!" Details now made perfect sense; that despite her inebriated state where she wasn't thinking clearly, she truly *did* intend the sincerity of that statement for me. Me!

At that very moment, my eye caught Samantha slowly sauntering up from behind, her face still bruised from the accident but looking so tender and fair, her azure dress with its light blue shoulder straps and turn-down collar that made her appear so meek and pure. Mr. Jensen tossed me a few coins and practically begged me to take the money and *finally* ask Samantha out for a quencher at the diner's soda fountain. The treat was on him, and he said this is the only exception he'd make to her grounding punishment for the next week. He continued on and said if I ever wanted to borrow his Skylark to take Samantha out on a respectable real date some weekend in the future, I was more than welcome to borrow it since he knew I didn't have a car of my own. Most meaningful of all, he said that he trusted me.

All of my fears were allayed at that moment. Mr. Jensen wasn't a mean or recalcitrant man as I had envisioned and was led to believe, but more of a gentle giant. I quickly gathered that he was simply trying to balance the stressful work challenges of increasing mine productivity and efficiency, transitioning his family to a new town, the fatherly demands of keeping his girls on the straight and narrow path, being a steadfast husband to his wife, and becoming an honorable and respected business leader in our town. It was a huge load all at once, and I empathized with the pressure of those pressing adult demands. I knew for certain now that not only would Samantha *never* be permitted to date Boone, but that she was truly interested in me after all—just neither of us had mustered up the courage and confidence to jump over that harrowing chasm for fear of rejection, of asking the other out.

With that, I shook his hand goodbye, and he hopped back in his car and drove off as I walked over to Samantha. She didn't say much; we just shared a long hug, and I could smell the sweet intoxicating scent of her perfume that I noticed she had freshly sprayed, knowing that she'd see me again that afternoon. I wanted her fragrance to permeate my sweater so I could hearken back and feel her near me long after this moment ended. She readily accepted my invitation to have that soda in the cafe.

We walked inside and sat at the lunch counter, and my mother, who was on shift, brought us two root beer floats that we enjoyed as Samantha and I laughed and chatted and got to know each other a little better. My heart welled with joy as I watched her coyly twist back and forth on her round stool, shyly smiling often as we talked.

"Remember at the homecoming dance those times that Boone and I were dancing and I said hello as we danced near you?" she asked.

"Absolutely, I remember," I replied.

"I wasn't having all that much fun, and I was kind of hoping you would cut in and ask for a dance," Samantha said.

"Well. . . that probably wouldn't have ended well," I replied, referring to Boone's size and demeanor. She nodded that she completely understood, and we shared several more laughs as we enjoyed our floats at the counter. She told me more details of the Pennsylvania Pocono coal town that she and her family had moved from, and how excited she was to paint and decorate her room in her new house. We talked for at least an hour, feeling more like long-lost friends than brand-new acquaintances by the end, and I relished how she lit up as she reminisced about her old hometown. The conversation flowed effortlessly, touching on a variety of topics, and things felt completely comfortable, real, and so much fun.

When we said our goodbyes around five o'clock, it didn't feel so much like a "goodbye" as a "see you soon." That quickly became a trait of our friendship. We never ended one moment that we were together without first longingly discussing the next moment when we could hopefully see each other again. I liked that, how nights and days spent apart from each other only made the moments that we were blessed to spend with each other even sweeter and more cherished. All the while, creating the excitement of having the next opportunity in mind of when we would likely get to share in a warm embrace, a hope to always look forward to.

Later that evening, when my mother's shift ended and she arrived home, she queried me regarding the girl I was with that afternoon and the man she spotted me talking with on the sidewalk. I told her everything, including how I had rescued Samantha from a car crash on Friday night, and how her dad wanted to personally thank me and encouraged me to develop a healthy and honorable friendship with his daughter.

Well. . . I might have embellished exactly what time I actually walked in the door in those wee hours of Sunday morning following the dance, but I didn't figure that part necessarily needed to be mentioned. . . All was good.

Chapter 11

The next day on my walk into the school building, I saw Boone at a distance.

When he noticed me, he came charging over in a huff. *Oh crud,* I thought. He brusquely accused me of trying to steal his woman, but I politely reminded him that Samantha is her own woman; she doesn't belong to anybody but her daddy and God. And when she's an adult, she still belongs to God and can make her own life decisions as an independent woman.

That quickly stopped Boone in his vexing tirade. I don't often throw God's name into my battles, although I silently hope and pray he's with me in each and every one. Skeptics often say that Christians use God as a crutch, which I suppose there's nothing wrong with when you recognize you're crippled without Him. But I think my bold statement of standing up for Samantha's independence got Boone's attention and he quickly backed down.

Boone then admitted that even the night he and Samantha were together, she brought up my name on more than one occasion, and he knew that the two of them would never last. He told me to have fun, and he quickly simmered down and went into the school. *Clearly he wasn't all that emotionally invested with her anyhow,* I thought to myself. Nor did he view her the way I felt deeply attracted to not only her physical beauty but her alluring, captivating, and adventurous personality.

As I walked into Mr. Smith's class, I smiled at Samantha, making full eye contact this time, and she warmly smiled back. I sat down at my desk behind her and playfully flipped her signature ponytail as I slid into my seat. She playfully whipped around like I was pestering her but shot me a quick flirty smile and a wink before turning forward again. Something about our friendship now felt comfortable, cozy, and fun. Gone were the tensions of wondering, the fear of doubt.

Mr. Smith continued his lesson on our local area's role in the Civil War. He then went on to teach that one of the most famous stories of our area is the legend of the *Tullahoma,* a locomotive owned by the Alabama & Tennessee Railroad. As the story goes, the *Tullahoma* was a locomotive that the railroad was trying to rush out of town with one final shipment of cotton for the harvest season prior to Thanksgiving 1863, the same year in which our town was founded.

However, just a few miles outside of town, the Yankees had advanced further south more quickly than anyone anticipated. They took positions on a ridge overlooking the railroad tracks and fired upon the defenseless crew as the train chugged northwest, claiming that the railroad was actually helping to fuel the Rebel cause, killing all crew members on board. The locomotive was disabled in the gunfire and sat idle on the tracks overnight. The next day, Confederate reinforcements arrived to overpower the Yankees and drove them back north toward Tennessee and away from Paxton and the rest of Northern Alabama.

After that, the engine was lost to history. Some people think the Yanks were able to commandeer the locomotive and drive it north before the Rebel forces arrived. Others think the engine was renumbered and renamed, dismantled, or scrapped for parts due to damage from the gunfight, being too great to repair. But up until those days, the sleek and speedy *Tullahoma* was a powerful workhorse through our town, making regular runs to Nashville, New Orleans, Atlanta, and other prominent cities throughout the South.

The raid on the *Tullahoma* had become a bit of a national legend over time, embedded in the broader narrative of the great Civil War. An interesting story, I suppose, a puzzle to piece together. Or perhaps nothing more than a legend with truth lost to time. As a history buff who enjoys a compelling mystery, discovering the truth would be incredible if it were even possible after all these years.

Chapter 12

That night at dinner, my mother asked what I learned in school that day, and I recounted the historical story that Mr. Smith had told us in class. She seemed to look on with particular intrigue. As a matter of fact, she recalled to me that in their younger years my father used to talk of an old locomotive engine that used to be housed on a siding track in the old railroad machine shed near our house.

When the Alabama & Tennessee Railroad went bankrupt shortly after WWII and not long after my father's death, my mother said that she assumed that the railroad had salvaged everything of value. All that remained scattered throughout the property were scraps of rusted iron and useless junk. She highly doubted that the locomotive of which my father spoke was *that particular engine,* which contributed so much to the local economy in those days and became an entertaining folktale and legend of our southern history. But there was always a chance.

At that moment, she stood up and walked over to my grandfather's original roll-top desk that had been in our family for decades and grabbed a letter that had recently arrived in the mail. From a distance, I could see that the letter had already been opened. Even from the other room, I could discern that the bold print on the cream-colored stationery hinted at the significance of the message contained within.

Changing subjects slightly as she held the letter in her hand, my mother explained to me that since the old railroad land we had been living on for so long was abandoned, she had written a letter to the Interstate Commerce Commission to petition for an official deed to our house under squatter's rights laws. Not that we were true squatters, but rather caretakers who had been maintaining our home and yard for nearly two decades. Hoping just to take full legal possession of our house and the acre of ground on which it stood, she read from the letter that the ICC granted that our house along with the entire sixty acres of old railroad property—to include the nearby machine shop that had been shuttered and locked behind barbed wire since the railroad went bankrupt in 1947—were ours free and clear.

"Wow, are you serious? That was a shock I wasn't expecting!" I said.

The ICC simply stated that while the house and grounds were ours, the federal government retained the rights to reactivate the long-forgotten rail line itself should it ever need to be requisitioned for national defense use in the future.

I was in complete disbelief. Such incredible news. Growing up in the years following WWII, I knew that more money and investment was being poured into the new-building boom across the country than into revitalizing older, forgotten places. Somehow, our town slipped through the cracks of this prosperity, and with its own economic struggles of a quickly depleting coal mine and mediocre cotton crop prices, it simply trudged along as just another lower-class rural southern town. Somehow, through a unique combination of oversight, economic stagnation, and revitalization, paired with the railroad bankruptcy years prior, my mother fortuitously became heir to a mortgage-free home and sixty-acre plot of land. It was like winning a huge lottery, and for once in our lives since my father had died, we wouldn't have to scrape to get by. We could finally feel as though we had a real financial footing and a bit of prosperity and security.

Mother explained that although the old locomotive repair shop, long since surrounded by weeds and brush behind a barbed wire fence, had likely been cleared out by the railroad before their bankruptcy seventeen years ago, there was still a chance some equipment or tools remained that we could sell for extra profit. I obviously knew of this building, knew of the barbed wire and gate surrounding it, and the subconscious part of my eye would see the building every day as I would come and go to our house. But to me it was just another building around town, and since it didn't belong to us up until now, I had never given much thought to the curiosity of what might be within. Now, though, I was instantly taken with the urge to explore every inch of it and what might be housed inside its ivy and wisteria overgrown walls.

It appeared that I would finally have that chance. *What was really in there anyhow, besides years' worth of cobwebs? Some old posters of trains would be cool.* With my mother's blessing, though, and now with legal proof that we were the owners of the entire abandoned Alabama & Tennessee Railroad facility overnight, she told me that tomorrow I could go over and explore the place.

Recalling back to the school lesson in Mr. Smith's class earlier that day, I wondered if perhaps some old documentation regarding the *Tullahoma* was still lying forgotten on a dusty shelf. Or, more emotionally intriguing, perhaps some old documents bearing the name and handwriting of my father were still tucked away in the recesses of the old repair shop. But for tonight, it was time to get some sleep.

That night, I lay awake for quite a while as I gazed out the window. The stars were shining brightly, and I was transported back to the night of the homecoming dance when I peered through the telescope in the science room at school. I felt stuck in a Sisyphus sort of existence in this rural town, dreaming of adventure as I peered through the window into the night sky like I had through the telescope at school several nights earlier. The stars and moon were the ever-present guiding lights of my restless spirit, no matter what the future held. Perhaps my mother's monumental news would be key in unlocking the chains and breaking free from this place. The very railroad property that kept my father employed here until he was drafted into the war would be the financial means I might be able to tap to one day escape this town.

Graduation was only a year and a half away, and although Mr. Smith often encouraged me to consider college, I knew that up until now my mother's financial situation would have precluded that possibility. Unless, perhaps, we could sell the adjacent rail yard—that is, if any company would actually buy it. It wasn't like Paxton had a bunch of industry or commercial businesses chomping at the bit to acquire more real estate. I also considered that the money from that would largely be the only retirement money my mother would have to live on for the rest of her life, beyond a meager Social Security check, since my father's military life insurance money had run out long ago. All wonders and apprehensions tumbled like a waterfall in my mind as I eventually drifted off to sleep.

Chapter 13

At school on Friday, I told Samantha that I had some incredible news to share and wanted to take her on an adventure. I knew that her bubbly, inquisitive, sprightly self would be up for exploring with me, and I relished the idea of going on an adventurous date together. Like *Robinson Crusoe* and the Hemingway books that sat on my nightstand, which allowed the restless boy in me to get lost in stories of adventure and exhilaration, I longed for the excitement of discovering whatever was in the old rail car repair shop. Samantha said that she was still grounded until this weekend, so she couldn't get together before then. She said that her family was going to the reservoir on Saturday for a picnic, but we agreed that on Sunday afternoon we would go on my yet-unrevealed adventure. She mentioned that her dad would love for me to join them for their family picnic if I was free on Saturday. Of course, any chance to see my little macushla was the only excuse I needed to cordially accept.

I knew that just getting into the old railroad shop was going to take some work just to access, so Friday after school I biked over to my brother's hardware and feed store for supplies. I would definitely need a hacksaw to cut through the locks on both the gate and the building itself since the keys had long since been lost to time. Charles greeted me when I walked through the door. He didn't appear as though our mother had yet clued him in on her newly acquired property deed to our house or the adjacent grounds. I kept that news quiet and simply said I needed to buy a hacksaw and a scythe for a project of cleaning up a bit around home. Thankfully, he didn't ask too many questions, since I didn't have too many answers, and he sold them to me at cost.

I quickly hightailed it out of there, and as I biked back home, I'm sure the townspeople thought I looked like the grim reaper with a saw in my hand and a scythe tucked under my arm. Then it dawned on me that it was nearly Halloween, so they probably thought I was just buying a few props for a party. Absent a black robe to complete the ghastly ensemble, luckily no townsfolk hollered at or stopped me to question what on earth I was doing as I quickly biked north toward home.

Dumping my bike by the front porch of the house and tossing my book bag on the steps, I walked over to the cyclone fence topped with barbed wire, which surrounded the red brick, rusty metal-roofed building within. *I feel as though I'm breaking into Fort Knox,* I thought to myself, still in disbelief that we now owned this acreage. But keeping my hopes in check, I quickly reminded myself that there was likely nothing actually in the building but junk and a few dead carcasses of animals that had somehow found their way inside but couldn't figure a way to scurry back out.

I began to saw the metal lock on the gate that connected to the rusty perimeter fence surrounding the facility, but after only ten strokes, the mechanism came apart, brittle with age. *That was pretty easy,* I thought. Setting the saw to the side, I began hacking the weeds that stood between the gate and the large round top metal door of the repair shop. As I whacked away at the weeds, being as loud and forceful as I could to chase away any snakes or vermin that might be hiding in the bluestem and fireweed grass, I followed the parallel iron rails underfoot that created a pathway of sorts, leading from the perimeter fence back to the large metal arch doors on the shop—doors large enough that when opened would allow for a railroad car or engine to enter for maintenance. I could envision the many locomotives and rail cars that would have been shuttled onto this track siding, and I wondered how many times my father had once walked this same path as he oversaw operations in the 1940s.

As I reached the door to the building itself, I could hear the hinges and siding creak as the breezy wind shuddered against the decades-old, long-forgotten building. The antique brass lock on this door was larger and heavier than the fence a hundred yards away, and the size and duty of the oversized lock made me wonder if it echoed the value of whatever treasure lay beyond its doors. This was the type of lock that you'd envision being on the latch of a pirate's chest or securing the cash in a Wells Fargo wagon as it crossed the open plains, but this one was even bigger. I gave it a stiff yank to see if it might fall apart the way the first lock had, but no luck. This one would take some actual sawing.

After fifteen minutes of tedious sawing with the hacksaw, the lock finally broke free. The door could now be opened for the first time in almost twenty years. Every impulse of my being badly wanted to open it and peek inside. I had that same evocative feeling of anticipation here and now in real life as I did when I read suspenseful *Hardy Boys* novels. But even more so, I really, really wanted to wait for Samantha because I craved having this shared adventure and exciting experience with my lovely, sweet girlfriend. Laying a hand upon the metal door for a moment and then stepping away, I retreated back home for the night.

Chapter 14

November was now upon us, and the crisp scent of dry leaves was solidly in the air. Samantha's family and I enjoyed a delicious picnic lunch on the bank near the reservoir that her mother had made, and in the distance, I could see a few other families doing the same. After lunch, her little sister Kathryn went down by the water's edge to play fetch with their black lab. Samantha and I grabbed our fishing poles and sat on the edge of the dock, talking, laughing, and being silly while her parents sat a short distance up the hill on their picnic blanket. She razzed me a bit for not telling her what this big adventure was that I had planned, but I told her that I wanted to build a little suspense. Plus, Sunday morning was church, and I was silently hoping that she would first join me there. Then in the afternoon, I promised that we could go on the mystery adventure. She agreed, and my heart swelled with the encouragement that we were progressively growing closer together with each passing day.

The rhythm of life in Alabama was marked by two things: the Friday night roar of the crowd at high school football stadiums and the Sunday morning hush of a church pew—and your tuchus had better be at each one if you were a true Southerner. It didn't matter who you were, how much money you made, what your skin color was, or if you were a blue-collar or a white-collar person, young or old. Most businesses in town were closed for both, and my brother's hardware store even posted early end-of-business hours on football Fridays since otherwise foot traffic would be dead. In the Deep South, faith and football were paramount then—and remain so today.

We had several churches in town, and my mother and I made Sunday morning services at Paxton Christian Church a high priority for as long as I can remember. Even as stroppy and obstinate as they were, Boone and Oliver would show up on rare occasions. As would their daddy, albeit a bit more boisterously, and as the congregation could attest, he usually did his worshiping while snoring from a back row.

Paxton Christian Church is characterized by its simple white clapboard construction and a prominent steeple that reaches high into the heavens above the front entrance. Colorful and vibrant stained glass panes cast a diverse patchwork of blended hues onto the modest rows of pews that lined the sanctuary. In the chancel beyond the altar, a rough-hewn cross of dark oak wood hangs prominently poised front and center. The church was historic and timeless and had been a longstanding fixture in our community for decades. Although relatively simple, I always felt a sense of inviting warmth every time I entered, a welcome respite from frenetic contemporary life outside its walls.

A true conservative Southern Bible-belt community, our townspeople were committed to their faith, and church pews were the sacred spaces for worship every Sunday morning. That's just the way people regarded their faith—trusting a higher power for blessings and guidance, listening to the message of the sermon, and offering a little sacrificial time of prayer and hymn singing in response.

Samantha met me outside the front of the church that morning. Since her dad had told me several days prior outside the Redbird Cafe that he stopped attending church as a result of the atrocities he had seen and experienced in the war, I was thankful that he at least allowed Samantha to attend with me so that I could introduce her to my faith. There was an eagerness in her demeanor, although I could also sense a little apprehension in her body language as she walked up to a church she had never been to before as the new girl in town. Small-town life can be a bit intimidating, the way the in-crowd sometimes glares and gawks at outsiders who are nestling into a new place, and I've observed that extending hospitality to newcomers is haphazard.

I gently took Samantha by the hand and led her up the steps and inside with me, and I could feel her clammy palms next to mine. Entering the sanctuary, I saw my mother, Charles, and his wife sitting in a pew near the front that looked a little tight for both of us to squeeze into, so Samantha and I quietly slipped into a row near the back. It felt so nice to hold her hand in mine, even if hers was a bit sweaty with nerves, and I think the security and confidence that I conveyed to her through my friendship and hospitality helped ease her trepidation. Worshiping alongside Samantha and singing "Blessed Assurance," "Bringing in the Sheaves," and "This Is My Father's World" was a beautiful moment, and I quietly thanked God in my heart for this moment that I had long since prayed for—the ability to grow closer to a beautiful and tender companion that I loved, someone who truly *got me,* while, all the time, both of us also growing closer to Him.

After church, everyone exited the building onto the front lawn and greeted Pastor Robert as we left. Samantha and I also said hello to my mother and brother, who were heading over to Charles' house for lunch. This was my first formal introduction of Samantha to my mother.

My mother had always said that any girl who loved me, she would love like a daughter, and I was so happy to see Samantha and my mom cordially hit it off well as they made small talk for a few minutes.

As we bid them adieu, Samantha and I walked back to my house, where I made us a couple of chicken salad sandwiches for lunch along with some southern sweet iced tea. By now, she was practically begging me for what adventure awaited us, playfully grabbing and shaking my shoulders as I washed up our lunch dishes. Jumping in to help me dry the dishes, I explained to her the extraordinary happenstance surrounding our new property deed that included ownership of the old locomotive shop nearby. I don't know that Samantha appreciated history in quite the same way as me, and she had no longstanding familial connection to this place the way that I did since my father worked here at one time. But nevertheless, her bubbly adventurous spirit excited me in wanting to share the moment together when we first opened the repair shop's long-shuttered doors. And to that fact, I could sense her eagerness.

As we left my house and walked over to the old building, I was taken with how much this moment with Samantha truly meant—I was developing a deeper fondness for my attraction toward her. The closer she and I grew together, the deeper sense of masculine protection I felt toward her in keeping her safe and looking after her. I loved the feeling of growing closer and sharing in this little adventure, because what is life after all but a series of many little adventures woven together over the fabric of time? As I so deeply desired to be her true gentleman and knight in shining armor, I considered it my job to carefully treasure the fact that God had lent Samantha into my care, and I would honor that trust by revering and protecting her in all we did together.

Being that it was early November and Halloween spooky season had just passed, I just hoped that any ghosts that resided in the building had moved on for a while. As we opened the first metal door to the shop, the rusty hinges creaked from the weight and movement of the doors that had not been opened in nearly twenty years.

The smell of musty air mixed with old oil and stale hydraulic fluid hit us almost immediately. Our eyes squinting and adjusting to the darker enclosed building from the bright sunlight, we stared dumbfounded and slack-jawed at the scene before us. I fully expected that the building would be nearly empty, but it felt as if we were stepping into a time capsule, and the men who had worked here had one day just walked away.

Drill presses and a belt sander were still in their place. An overhead crane beneath the triangular saw-tooth roof rested motionless with a giant hook hanging beneath as if frozen in time. Oil and paint cans were scattered throughout the room, as were tools of every shape and size. But most significantly, off to the right side, I could see the ancient frame of an old steam engine that resembled one straight out of *The Harvey Girls.*

The rail car repair shop was preserved as a snapshot of a bygone era, a relic of the past as if just suddenly abandoned in the mid-1940s the day the railroad went bankrupt. We were both completely speechless.

"I can't believe the railroad never cleaned this place out?!" I exclaimed to Samantha.

I suppose the Alabama and Tennessee Railroad just went bankrupt one day, and when no creditors came after this building, likely opting for operational railroad cars and other rolling stock instead, this small town facility was overlooked and eventually fell through the cracks. It was just sealed and forgotten as if a time capsule. A chapter closed.

We slowly walked over to the hulking behemoth of a time-fettered locomotive engine. Samantha nestled in tight and clung to my arm as if we were staring face to face with an iron monster that could suddenly awake without warning, which I had to assure her was neutralized and rendered inert before she'd approach any closer.

As her new beau, I liked the primal feeling of being her protector. Her safeguard. Her fearless leader. I got the feeling that she had never had a boyfriend who was like that before, and perhaps Boone wasn't the first troublemaker with reckless abandon she had gotten mixed up with as she searched for male companionship. Nevertheless, as a bookworm and nerdy kid that most girls overlooked, I was beginning to like this new feeling of someone looking up to and entrusting me. Samantha was certainly someone whom I deeply cared for and no doubt was completely smitten with and would protect at all costs.

I reached out to touch the rusted old engine, and it was strange connecting with such a powerful machine that practically sat in my own backyard, that at one time pulled countless tons of cargo and passengers to distant places all over the country. Places I could only dream of visiting. But in this moment, it sat quiet and motionless as a forgotten vestige of time, with only the weight of spiders and cobwebs upon its wheels.

I hadn't even thought of it since I was just caught up in the moment, but Samantha then reminded me of the legend that Mr. Smith had recalled in class surrounding the *Tullahoma. Could this be it?!* No way, that was either a fantastical story, or else it had long since been recycled for metal during the scrap drives during WWII. This engine's paint was all gone, stripped and flaked away by years of neglect, age, and evidence that at some point, someone had begun actually restoring it back to its mid-1800s luster.

There was no way that we could readily identify an engine number or name due to its rough mechanical state. Missing also were its bell, headlamp, and cowcatcher. It would be hard to determine exactly what we were looking at, but in any case, we recognized the enormity of our immense find. Heck, even if it wasn't worth a dime—which I was sure it certainly had to be to somebody—it was just cool that we had rediscovered it after all these years.

I climbed up into the cab and reached back to lend a hand to Samantha, who readily climbed up behind me. From this vantage point, we had an all-new perspective of the old machine shop. I could see long workbenches, rows of tools, and what appeared to be an office at the far end of the building. The control cab of the locomotive had a myriad of gauges and dials, housed in beautiful brass frames, but they were in dire need of polishing. I also recognized the throttle and brake levers as we continued investigating the engineering controls, all the while batting away years' worth of cobwebs as we explored.

All of a sudden, we heard the screech of a raccoon that popped its head out from the coal tender behind us that was coupled to the engine. I think it was just as startled to see us as we were to see it! Probably the first humans the rodent had ever laid eyes upon. We jumped backward, and in the commotion of excitement, a flurry of pigeons we hadn't noticed before, sitting on an overhead pipe, fluttered out a broken skylight and into the air above, their wings making the unmistakable slapping and clapping sound that only pigeons do as they flutter upward. The entire workshop seemed to come alive all at once, so I jumped off the engine and onto the concrete floor below, reaching back an arm to help Samantha down. As quickly as we could, we scurried out of there. That was enough of a reconnaissance mission for one day.

We slammed shut the door to the building and loosely hung the lock that I had cut through the eyelet to lightly secure the doors. Resting our backs against the doors as if resealing a spooky tomb and mentally trying to make sense of everything we had just observed and encountered, we then burst out laughing about the raccoon, now that we were far removed from any danger. Taking quick stock of what we had seen, we knew that there were tools, a locomotive engine and coal tender, and an unexplored office area we didn't yet explore. There was much more to investigate, so we gathered our thoughts and decided that the best person to relay our findings to would be Mr. Smith to see if he could help us make sense of all we discovered.

Chapter 15

After quickly finishing my newspaper route on Monday morning, I headed into school, hoping Mr. Smith would be there early preparing for the school week ahead. He was, and much to my delight, he seemed curious and deeply interested in what we had discovered as I excitedly talked a mile a minute in a torrent of words, explaining our initial findings to him. Although skeptical that it was actually the *Tullahoma* housed inside, nevertheless, the three of us made plans after class that afternoon to show him our find and to see if he could better explain what we were looking at.

Since the autumn sun dips early in November and dappled shadows grow long through the drapery of willow branches, we knew that we wouldn't have much time to explore the shop with Mr. Smith before darkness would be afoot. Luckily, I ran by home on our way to grab a couple of flashlights so that we could see a bit better as we raced against the setting sun and a cool, cloudy sky. Opening the door, this time a bit more cautious of what critters could be lurking inside, it appeared that the coast was clear.

Mr. Smith's jaw dropped as he saw the ancient iron horse at the far end of the machine shed. He was even more fascinated than we were, given his breadth of understanding and far superior knowledge of history than either Samantha or I possessed. Samantha went over to the long row of workbenches and started to decipher what all of the tools were and what they might have been used for, while Mr. Smith clamored on all four sides of the locomotive, studying its design, its shape, the suspension of the undercarriage, and its overall condition.

Eager to investigate the shop's office, I made that my first point of exploration. Turning the door handle and fighting my way through cobwebs and dust, I walked into a time capsule of an early-century machinist's office. On the single desk before me were stacks of blueprints and schematics, with the names of old engines like the *Susquehanna,* the *Columbian,* and the *Nebraskan* written in architectural lettering in the header. There were diagrams of locomotive drive wheels, crank rods, and Pullman passenger car plottings. I could still make out the sweet aroma of isopropanol and methanol on the pages of mimeograph drafting paper. Even after all of the forgotten years, the protection and security of the interior office had a way of staving off the deleterious effects of Alabama humidity and moth damage after such a long passage of time.

As I opened the filing cabinet, the musty smell of paperwork flooded out. None of the documents appeared to have any particular significance, just routine record keeping. *There's got to be more here*, I thought to myself. *You don't just have a locomotive parked in a machine repair shop without more to the story.*

By now I was thankful that I had brought my flashlight as I returned to the desk and began thumbing through the drawers themselves. The glass windows in the sawtooth roof above the main floor of the shop cast a bit of sunlight into the machine shop, but through the additional dusty glass panes of the interior office itself, lighting was pretty faint. I opened the upper drawer on the desk, and there were pencils, metal rulers and protractors, a few large alligator paper clips, and other mundane office supplies. Nothing of particular value was spotted except for a few old three-cent postage stamps. Being that this was the shop's office, I was confident that it would definitely be where all of the important paperwork and secrets were kept.

As I opened the lower box drawer of the desk, I found a large, brown leather-bound notebook that was tied up with taut strings. Opening it up, several photographs and loose-leaf notes tumbled out. Picking them up off the dusty floor and setting the notebook itself on the desk, I paused for a moment when I instantly recognized my father in one of the black-and-white photographs, proudly standing in front of a locomotive. I was mesmerized that I was actually holding a picture of him in my hands. There was a name on that train, and I squinted to make it out, as the paint on the locomotive in which it was stenciled in the photo was faded and peeling. Holding my flashlight at just the right angle, it read. . . *Tullahoma!* My heart raced as if it were about to burst out of my chest. This train looked remarkably like the engine outside the window of the office, though the engine in the repair shop didn't bear any name, and much of the paint had at some point been sanded away in preparation for restoration and repainting just as Samantha and I had discovered yesterday.

Seeing an image of my father made my eyes instantly well up. Although I never met him, we had several photographs throughout our home with his image, including one in his military dress uniform, so I instantly recognized his image. I envisioned him in his role at the shop, a hard-working stationmaster who was responsible for running this large operation, as well as being a deeply devoted husband and father with one son nearly eight years old and another soon on the way, prior to his military draft.

As I choked back tears, my thoughts instantly turned to regretting the war, that it even had to happen in the first place. It seemed so distant and impersonal since it was fought in lands so far away and removed from Alabama—a place that could have been home for our happy family. So much life yet to live was gone in a moment, and my anger burned at the thief of battle that had destroyed the balance of our potential family. The war robbed us and stole time and memories that he and I could have shared throughout my youth, something a photograph could never exchange. My father looked to be in his mid- to late-20s in the photograph, so I knew that it couldn't have been taken more than a few short months prior to his draft into the Marines. Wiping a couple of tears from my eyes, I slipped the photo into my pocket so that I could show it to my mother later that night.

Turning my attention back to the binder, I saw several old photos of the *Tullahoma* again. There were all sorts of handwritten notes about the history of its early life as an operating engine. I instantly recognized my father's handwriting on these pages. It was the same familiar script I'd seen countless times in the love letters he'd sent my mother during his time in boot camp and while serving overseas. I'd secretly discovered these letters years ago in a box at home and often found myself rereading them as I yearned to learn more of the father whom I never met.

Choked up and reading deeper into his handwritten memos, I was able to construct a bit of background in this forgotten story. Piecing together old newspaper clippings that it appeared my father had researched and assembled, the narrative seemed to indicate that following the Union raid on the rail line, Union troops were never able to commandeer the locomotive or the rest of its cargo to head back to the North. They had killed the engineer, and none of the other soldiers knew how to operate the train. The day after the raid, Confederate troops pushed the Union forces back to the North, and the locomotive was disconnected from the rest of the train it was pulling and towed back to town to be repaired or later scrapped.

Although the locomotive was desperately needed for the war effort, virtually all of the men who possessed the knowledge and skill to repair it were off fighting in the Civil War, so it sat idle for years. In the reconstruction years following the Civil War, new locomotive technology came along, rendering the *Tullahoma* obsolete. The locomotive became a shut-in vestige of years gone by as it slowly rusted away in a corner of the rail yard for decades under the hot Alabama sun. Decades passed. Then in the late 1930s my father and his crew recognized the significance of this historical artifact and towed it inside the shop's second repair bay that was rarely used for a slow restoration, as time and money allowed.

Where had I heard this sort of story before, I thought. Time has a fickle way of marching on, as new technologies and innovations replace old ones. It similarly echoed the story of how the new diesel rail line bypassed Paxton, and the fate of our town's steam train era was rendered obsolete and left to die. So was the fate of this engine in its era, and it was far too damaged in the raid to ever be put back into service. After the war, it was cheaper to produce new locomotives than to salvage and preserve older ones. We often feel pressured to adapt to new technologies, lest we be left behind. Yet, it's the past we strive to outrun that ends up fueling future innovation.

When WWII started and there were talks of scrap metal drives, my father's notes outlined that he had orchestrated a plan to hide the rusted locomotive out of the sight of prying eyes of whoever might come looking to melt it down. Scrap metal drives galvanized the home front during WWII, allowing ordinary citizens across the country the chance to feel like they were making a firsthand difference in the war effort by promoting patriotism and unity in their communities. I think my father felt that, in saving this historic locomotive from the blast furnace, he was also promoting patriotism and preserving history in his own unique way.

Holding a flashlight in my hand as I continued on, his notes detailed that over the next few years, he and the men in the shop worked on its restoration. The notes detailed that the crew rebuilt and restored the chassis, pistons, and rods, sanding and scraping rust away. All of the old paint was sanded clean and all of the brass gauges were repaired and reinstalled. Even the bell, whistle, and headlamp were removed, cleaned, and repaired, and were ready to be reinstalled as soon as it was repainted and the restoration finalized. His notes were meticulous, and it was clear that his love for preserving the past and a piece of not just local—but national—history was of clear importance to him.

I knew that by the end of WWII, many of the machinists and laborers who worked in this building were also sadly killed or severely injured during the war. After the war, when it was clear that the writing was on the wall and that the railroad would soon go bankrupt, the remaining men were laid off or transferred elsewhere. It was as if the entire railroad operation that literally built Paxton out of nothing into a stop on the early steam railroad line was completely forgotten on the other end of a once-prominent bell curve of prosperity. A *Flying Dutchman* of sorts, now rudderless, lonely, and abandoned.

Speaking of forgetting, I almost forgot that Mr. Smith and Samantha were still outside the office door in the main shop.

"Guys, come quick!" I heard Samantha yell.

I looked out the office window toward Mr. Smith, who had found a pad of paper and looked like he was taking meticulous axiological notes as he studied the locomotive. I couldn't see Samantha from my vantage point, but I leapt up out of the chair and dashed out into the main shop.

"Look at what I found!" Samantha exclaimed as Mr. Smith and I reached the place in the shop where Samantha was standing. She was crouched down underneath the long workbench and had just slid out two large, heavy crates marked *Tullahoma*. Mr. Smith and I bent down to help lift them from the concrete floor and onto the main workbench. I found a pry bar and removed the top to the crates, and we both stood over her while she peeled back layers of embrittled brown paper within each crate to reveal its contents. *Tools maybe? Bolts or other hardware?* One was longer and more rectangular, and the other more cube-shaped.

Mr. Smith reached into one as Samantha and I simultaneously peered into the other. We could hardly contain ourselves—inside the two boxes were the whistle and bell from the *Tullahoma*. Mr. Smith and I high-fived each other, and I leaned over to give Samantha a big hug, both of us by now covered in a layer of dust and grime and decades-old locomotive grease. "Awesome find!" I said.

I reached under the bell and could feel the knocker and tapped it into the side of the bell. *Clunk!* It sounded muffled, since we were holding onto the bell at the same time as we were ringing it, but we could still hear the metal timbre that once adorned this locomotive and would greet passengers as the iron machine rolled into each town.

Samantha leaned over the whistle, carefully angling her breath to capture the faintest metallic pitch of sound as she blew into the bevel. I could imagine the sound as it would have once pierced the air, a note heard by countless passengers rushing to board the train. I couldn't help but picture those hurried scenes: suitcases in hand, porters lifting chests of personal wares and mail and other cargo into the boxcars and Pullman coaches. Passengers would be eagerly yearning to reach loved ones as they bid farewell to others, all accompanied by the distinctive wail of the train whistle as it departed each station in a frenetic haste. Clearly, the bell and whistle were removed and tucked safely away during the early restoration process stages to protect their fragility.

Discovering this historic locomotive, for which my father had clearly held a deep affinity, felt like an adventurous way for me to connect with him. It was a way to bridge the gap between myself and a man I never had the chance to meet in this lifetime. A profound longing compelled me to learn more about my father's life. Rediscovering the locomotive on which he once worked, and for which he held such a great passion, felt like the missing coupler that would finally bridge us together.

I then shared with the two of them what I had discovered in the office, pulling out the old photo of my father standing in front of the train. They were both amazed that it had survived all of these years. Mr. Smith shared that he had found the original manufacturing data plate on the ceiling of the *Tullahoma's* cab, confirming what we all knew now that was true—this was the actual engine that was written of in history books that played an instrumental part in the Civil War. It was fun sharing each of our findings with one another as we collaborated on our adventure toward the common goal of unearthing this exciting find—as if we had each found rooms with different sarcophagi all within the umbrella of the same giant pyramid.

Chapter 16

After we left the rail car shed for the night, Mr. Smith gave Samantha a ride home. I walked back to my house. The sky was almost completely dark by now, but gazing toward home, I could see a few lights inside and could faintly smell supper cooking so I knew that my mother was home from her shift at the cafe. Opening the door to step inside, I pulled the photograph of my father out of my pocket and gracefully reached around in front of her to present it as she faced the stove, her back to me.

Pausing for a second as she looked upon the picture, she instantly stopped stirring what was in the pot and turned around to meet me. "Where on earth did you get that?!" she asked. I told her everything we had discovered in the machine shed and how I had found it in a stack of notes and other documents. Evidently, one of my father's railroad employees had snapped the picture of him shortly before he was drafted and deployed to the Pacific. A wave of grief washed over her as she brought a hand to her mouth. Tears welled up in her eyes as she reminisced about the life she and my father had shared and the profound empty feeling and loneliness she had felt since his death.

I thought a lot about that moment and the fact that my mother never particularly had much of a desire to come over to the machine shop during our first adventures of its initial uncovering. In a way, I don't think she had ever grieved sufficiently. Although the pain of my father's death should have healed with the passing of time, I think that in certain little moments throughout each day, things still remained all too real. After she heard the news and he was returned home on a military train car and buried a few weeks later, I think she recognized in that moment that there was little time to mourn. My brother was seven years old and about to turn eight, and I was soon to be born myself; there was no way to press the pause button on life. With no siblings in the area and grandparents who had gone before us, she had to navigate through life as a young widow the best she could.

Women were tough back then; they mourned in their own private way, and nobody really discussed their feelings of grief. I think my mother poured herself into as much work at the Redbird Cafe as she could handle. It was a way of escapism from her stressful storm cloud of figuring out where she would live if the railroad should suddenly kick us out of our company-owned home and the concern about what she would do for money once my father's wartime life insurance ran out. There was no time to feel sorry for herself, and with strong recollections of the hard times of the Dust Bowl and Great Depression, she had to maintain a stiff upper lip and fully invest in pressing on with life, despite her husband no longer being in the picture.

I think the other part of her hesitation to come over to the repair shop wasn't that she was trying to distance herself from the connection to my father, but that it was her way of giving me permission to make that personal connection with him myself, since I didn't have the luxury of developing one with him throughout my childhood. She recognized it was my way of knowing him on a certain plateau for our shared love of history and machines and "guy stuff," where he and I could bond and connect now, even if he wasn't here in the present. I suspect perhaps she knew more about his passion for saving that old, rusted steam engine than she ever admitted. Seeing my own enthusiasm and zeal for the project —now that we owned the abandoned rail yard and everything within—must have felt like her way of allowing me to carry on his legacy.

The next few days before and after school, Mr. Smith and I earnestly discussed our next course of action. He and I definitely agreed that we should preserve this engine, a restoration that was well on its way, thanks to early efforts by my father. We just weren't sure if we should announce it to the town quite yet, so the two of us, along with Samantha, agreed to keep things under tight wraps.

Flipping several pages on his calendar in the classroom, Mr. Smith brought to my attention that the town's centennial celebration would be the following June—just over a year and a half away. He proposed a fantastical idea: what if we were able to fully restore this locomotive and present it to the town in time for the centennial? After all, not only would 1963 be a celebration of Paxton's one hundredth birthday, but it would be almost one hundred years since the Union raid on the locomotive, catapulting it into the history books.

I was instantly captivated by the challenge of achieving this goal and the incredible surprise it would bring to our town if we succeeded. It would be a monumental undertaking. We all three agreed to pursue this restoration as a joint endeavor, keeping our efforts under strict secrecy as we went.

Chapter 17

Christmas 1961 was a joyous time, and I was happy to have a few weeks of rest and relaxation. School had let out a few days before, and the sweet freedom of winter break stretched ahead of us until early January. On Christmas Eve, Mr. Jensen allowed me to borrow his Buick, and I picked Samantha up for a fancy date to go and see *To Kill a Mockingbird* at the theater. Well, the date wasn't all that ritzy, I suppose, but I did dress in a gray sport coat and skinny black tie to present myself more formally. When I picked Samantha up, she was wearing a beautiful aubergine dress from Newberry's that her folks had given her for Christmas, which her mother relented and permitted her to open a day early so that she could wear it on our Christmas Eve date and to church later that evening.

It made me so incredibly happy that her family realized how much we meant to each other and how close we were growing. In those days, it wasn't uncommon for high school couples to end up getting engaged and married, and I think her parents saw that, with my academic aptitude in school and work ethic in maintaining my daily paper route, I would likely be a college boy in another year and a half. I was good for Samantha, and she was right for me. The idea of a future together loomed large, but the reality was that my own future remained uncertain, as I was still adrift, unsure of my post-graduation plans. Even if I managed to get into a good college, the financial burden was still a significant obstacle yet to overcome.

When we arrived at the *Strand* downtown, I quickly put the car in park and ran around to the passenger side to open the door for Samantha, reaching for her hand as she gracefully stepped onto the curb. We were able to park near the entrance, and it was fun to pretend that we were going into a Hollywood premiere at Grauman's Chinese Theatre the way the bright marquee lights danced and flickered in the background. After we picked up a couple of Cokes and a big bag of popcorn from the concession stand, we headed to our seats. I settled in, placing an arm behind Samantha's neck and giving her a quick peck on the cheek just as the lights began to dim. She rolled her eyes in playful contempt and shy disdain before quickly returning the kiss. Then, shoving a handful of popcorn into her mouth as she looked straight ahead to face the screen, she snuggled into the crook of my arm as we anticipated the start of the movie.

As I sat there watching this coming-of-age film, one that took place right here in Alabama, I reflected on the pointed disparity of good versus evil and social inequality right here in Paxton. I couldn't get rid of the thought of Boone and Oliver, who lived in a ramshackle cabin on that former plantation just outside of town. Other than their success on the football field, they were both looked upon by much of the town as outcasts—far below the other townsfolk. Despite the town's overall economic hardship, the family stood out as markedly different, a subset within an overall lower-class community. Their life circumstances and demeanor perpetually drew scornful glances and hushed criticisms from the townspeople. I thought of how, even on Sunday mornings, the relatively rare Sabbath days when they did show up, they typically shuffled in late and ducked out right as the church service ended so they wouldn't have to interact or converse with anybody.

A perplexity arose: were they looked down upon because of their social class and the way that they talked and dressed, or did they treat other people with contempt because they never received one ounce of compassion or understanding in their entire lives? The dichotomy bemused me as I rationalized there has always been righteousness and wickedness in the world, rich folks and poor folks, just and unjust, respect and disdain. While the specific forms of social and racial inequality differed somewhat from the movie, I recognized parallels to the marginalization and ostracism I've witnessed within my own community.

My mother and I were not rich by any standard, and I wondered why we seemed to have escaped the same contempt. Could it be because we lived within the city limits? Or that my mother had worked for more than two decades at the town diner and everyone knew us and because of that familiarity had taken a liking to us? Was it because my father, a local wartime hero who died giving his life to protect our freedoms, was a bit of a hometown celebrity? Perhaps it was simply because my mother always raised Charles and me to treat everyone we came across with kindness, courtesy, and respect, and those Christian virtues tended to elicit similar goodness in others? The thoughts permeated my mind throughout the film.

It was a fun little date, even if the themes were heavy-hitting, and as soon as the movie ended, we headed back to Samantha's house. Samantha, along with her sister Kathryn and me, hopped in the back of the car while her mom and dad took the front seat as we drove to church for the candlelight Christmas Eve service. It was a beautiful service where we sang "The First Noel," "Away in a Manger," and "Go Tell It on the Mountain" amid the soft glow of several dozen flickering candles. I smiled as I looked over at Samantha, watching the gentle candlelight and shadows dance across her sweet face. I was happy that her parents had also joined us for this special Christmas Eve service, even though it was the only church service I ever saw them attend.

Afterward, I hopped a ride home with my mother, but with permission from her, I invited Samantha to come over to our house the next day on Christmas afternoon for dessert. I recognized that her family would want her home for their own gift-giving, celebrations, and family traditions. However, I hoped to steal her away for an hour so she could join us for some pie and coffee. She asked her folks, who said it would be fine. My heart was happy; this would be our first Christmas together, even if it was only for a short mid-afternoon moment.

Chapter 18

When Samantha came over Christmas Day, my mother, Charles, his wife Millie, and little Cordelia were in the middle of opening presents in our modest living room. Well, Cordelia was mostly eating the wrapping paper, but at least she was enjoying herself. I had found a scrappy little volunteer cedar tree along the back fence line of the sprawling rail yard perimeter, which I had cut and dragged to the house and adorned with tinsel and lights the week before. I presented Samantha with a silver heart necklace that I had specially picked out from the Sears & Roebuck catalog with my newspaper route money. She loved it and equally admired the chain upon which it hung. I told her that so long as she and I were dating, she would always have my love, and this necklace was to signify that I would always be hers if she carried me close.

I didn't ask for any special presents myself, as I've always been more of a simple and practical gift person and value time and special moments as much as I appreciate tangible items to unwrap. However, knowing of monumental tasks ahead with the locomotive restoration, Samantha unexpectedly presented me with a pair of genuine cowhide work gloves. She looked over at Charles, who winked. She told me later that she had purchased them from his store and he had personally helped her select them. Trying them on, I was ecstatic that she had taken the time to choose such a thoughtful and functional gift for me. My hand fit like a glove inside of them—pun intended—and the soft and malleable leather meant that I'd still have plenty of dexterity when using them. They were perfect and would be great for working both on the locomotive restoration as well as jobs around the house. I thanked her dearly for such a thoughtful present, and she just blushed, her cute dimples revealed in her tender smile.

Just then, there was a knock on the front door, which caught us all off guard. I stood up to walk over to open the front door, and standing on the porch was Mr. Smith. When Samantha heard me greet him, she got up from the living room and came over to say hello, too. We were both surprised to see him on Christmas Day, of all times, but he handed each of us a box. Both were of the same shape, long and rectangular, wrapped in brown paper with a simple cloth bow.

We stepped out onto the covered porch and sat down on the wooden bench and unwrapped each of our boxes. Inside were pairs of durable gray denim coveralls, and Mr. Smith stated that he wanted to give us each a special gift for inviting him along on our railroading adventure. If we were going to restore a vintage Civil War locomotive, he said we needed the right clothes in which to do it. We both wholeheartedly thanked him as we each held up our pairs in front of ourselves to gauge how they'd fit. Hearing us outside on the front porch, my mother hollered at me to invite Mr. Smith inside for dessert and coffee, and he readily accepted. I took both of our gifts and quickly tucked them out of sight inside the coat closet so that my brother and his wife wouldn't start asking a bunch of questions since we had yet to inform anyone of our exciting find, still opting to keep our endeavor a secret.

Mr. Smith said that he didn't want to impose, but that he'd enjoy one quick cup of coffee and then be on his way. I was surprised he wasn't with his family on Christmas Day, but I knew he wasn't married. He later explained that his family lived in Baltimore, and he had chosen to spend Christmas alone rather than incur the expense of traveling. Secretly, I think he was eager to return to the rail car shop and begin our monumental project: the clandestine restoration of a national treasure that nobody outside of these walls even knew existed.

We all migrated into our small kitchen where my mother's cherry pie awaited us, joined by Millie's apple cobbler. I brewed some strong black coffee, and we enjoyed a delightful afternoon, savoring the desserts and engaging in lively conversation surrounding mundane local news and gossip. An AM radio softly played Perry Como's "Home for the Holidays" in the background. I observed my mother and Mr. Smith conversing with ease, and I began to wonder if her invitation had a deeper purpose than simple Southern hospitality. However, as a teacher and a waitress, I also knew they were both accustomed to engaging with the public, so I assumed it was nothing more than friendly conversation. Regardless, I wouldn't have minded if there was more to it, as long as they were both happy.

As Mr. Smith prepared to leave, Samantha and I walked with him to the front porch as she had mentioned the need to head home herself. The three of us agreed to meet at the rail car shed the following morning and spend the next two weeks of our Christmas break working on the slow and tedious but exciting restoration process. As we both thanked

Mr. Smith again for his kind gifts, I gave Samantha a hug, and she was on her way as well.

Chapter 19

The following morning, our first order of business was to determine how we could get electricity working in the shop. A concern was the possibility of rodents having chewed through the asbestos wiring after two decades of neglect, the last time anyone had set foot in the building. There were overhead green enamel work lights, and I wondered if the shop was actually on the same electric line as our house since, at one time, the railroad paid the utility bills for both. Finding an old fuse panel at the back of the shop next to the office, I couldn't even tell if the fuses that were installed were in operable condition, given years' worth of deterioration and corrosion. On a nearby shelf, though, I found a box of brand new fuses, and, carefully wearing my new leather gloves that Samantha had given me the day prior, I popped out the old blown ones and sandwiched new ones between the couplers.

Here goes nothing, I thought as I threw the Frankenstein-sized breaker, not knowing what I was even doing or if it had a prayer's chance of working.

Whoosh! The sound of electricity surged through the old wiring with a hum. *No fires!* was my first thought as I glanced throughout the shop and looked for the unmistakable sight or smell of sparks and smoke. Incredibly, a third of the overhead lights in the shop came on, so I knew we had full power. It would just be a matter of finding some spare bulbs to replace the burned-out ones above. A radio on the workbench that I had not even noticed before came to life with the introduction of electricity and began blaring the crisp, unmistakable voice of an Elvis Presley Christmas song from the last station it was tuned to. *Awesome, we will even have music to listen to while we work!* I thought to myself.

Samantha and Mr. Smith arrived shortly thereafter, and Samantha was wearing her gray overalls that matched mine. "Now we really look like a team!" I said. She smiled, and, flexing her little arms as if putting up her dukes, said her Rosie the Riveter persona could take me on with no problem. We both laughed for a moment as I pretended to playfully spar with her, and then it was time to get to work.

Mr. Smith laid out a bunch of plans and diagrams for this particular model of locomotive that he had requested through the library in Huntsville. It was incredible, seeing the U. S. patents and all sorts of schematics that would aid us as we capitalized on our break from school to get a jump start on our reconstruction efforts. Thankfully, my father's notes aided us as well. He had done a meticulous job cataloging all of the work he had previously begun.

Mr. Smith and I spent the next several days sanding with an electric angle iron sander. Flakes and bits of paint chips flicked off and littered the concrete floor and lead dust filled the air. When we finished with the engine, we moved on to the coal tender. Samantha also tasked herself with determining if we had the proper hardware we needed to reattach the whistle and bell, and while those components would be the last to piece together in our restoration efforts, I smiled at her alacrity when she jumped at that particular undertaking that called to her.

The cowcatcher was one piece of the puzzle that was completely missing, having presumably been salvaged for another project years prior. It was also quite possible that the metal frame was removed after the gunfight, when the locomotive was towed back to town. Using more old photographs as our guides and scrap metal found throughout the shop, Mr. Smith and I painstakingly cut, heated, and bent the metal over a blacksmith's anvil to conform to the similar look of the cowcatcher in the photographs we had at our disposal.

Slaving away the next two weeks of Christmas break, the three of us would work wherever we could on whatever project caught our eye that needed doing in our spare time. Sanding. Scraping. Sweeping up our mess. Coughing up gunk and often stopping to blow our noses. The work never ended, but we felt as though we were making progress.

Chapter 20

Soon enough, the bleak gray days of winter gave way to the warmer, longer days of spring. One Saturday afternoon while we were working, my mother entered the shop for the first time. We saw her approach through the huge open doorway where the rails exited out of the shop and into the rail yard. We all simultaneously halted our work and looked up. Her eyes swept across the building, surveying the scene much like I'm sure we did when we entered for the first time.

"So this is the big project you three are working on?" she queried us.

"Yes, and hi!" I said, still surprised to see her poke her head in since she had seemed largely detached from our entire endeavor up until now. "Well, Dad had started much of this project from what his journal revealed, repairing the boiler, installing new wheels, and welding patches onto the undercarriage. Thankfully, because those parts would have been too big for us to have completed on our own. Most of our work has been sanding and scraping to prep for paint."

She didn't reply much, mostly nodding and taking it all in as a host of old memories likely came flooding back. She held out her hands and had a plate with a big stack of chocolate chip cookies and three bottles of pop.

"I figured you three could use a break; you've been working so hard on this," she said.

Thanking her for the treats, I used the edge of a vise on the workbench to crack open two bottles for Samantha and me, and Mr. Smith popped his open on a piece of iron trim of the locomotive. We thanked her for the treats, and while Mr. Smith and my mother began to chat, Samantha and I retreated to the far end of the shop. We found a couple of round wooden stools to sit on and rest, wiping years of dust and grime from our hands onto our overalls as best we could before we dove into the cookies.

I suspected my mother wanted to ask Mr. Smith adult-to-adult, "How are these kids doing? They're not causing you any trouble, are they?" and things of that nature. But it was also more than likely she coyly appreciated his company. I still couldn't tell if there were any feelings or connection there, for either of them. At least not how I fell head-over-heels for Samantha in a passionate, hearts-aflame way. I suppose their connection had more to do with Mr. Smith's taking a liking to me and the closeness he and I shared as we worked on this project together.

While many of the other guys in my class bonded with their fathers over baseball or car repairs, Mr. Smith, in a way, filled a void, offering the paternal guidance and companionship I longed for. This locomotive restoration was our bond. I suppose my mother saw this connection as admirable in her eyes and one she was thankful I had found. Since she and my high school teacher were of similar age— the same age my late father would have been—the two of them shared a connection somewhere in between friendship and courtship. The two definitely lit up brighter than lightning bugs in the northern Alabama foothills whenever they were near each other; that much was for certain.

I appreciated the chance myself just to sit and admire Samantha for a few moments. We had been working so hard most of these days, completely greasy and grimy, that I had forgotten to take a moment to appreciate the hard-working, beautiful young woman that she was. We had been seriously dating for nearly six months now, and every day I was truly falling more in love with her. In her gray overalls and her braided hair, I admired the strength and determination she exuded. A powerful young lady, but in a petite and slender maidenly frame.

Despite the grime and dirt that might have obscured her appearance to others, I found her exquisite, her appearance irrelevant to my admiration and perception of her beauty. In no way did it make her unattractive, and somehow it even had the opposite effect on me, since through our hard work together we were growing closer as partners. I was equally thankful that she took a long liking to me in spite of my own filthy appearance of sweat and dust, and it didn't bother her to sit down and enjoy a few minutes of rest with me.

As we were enjoying our little break, a song came on the AM radio that was sitting atop the long metal workbench, and we both paused to soak in its lyrics:

I bless the day I found you
I want to stay around you
And so I beg you, let it be me

Don't take this Heaven from one
If you must cling to someone
Now and forever, let it be me

Each time we meet, love
I find complete love

Without your sweet love
What would life be?

So never leave me lonely
Tell me you love me only
And that you'll always, let it be me

"Hey, I really love this song!" Samantha said to me.

I had heard it several times before; the old Everly Brothers song had been on the radio for a couple of years at this point, but I guess I hadn't soaked in the depth of its lyrics until now.

"It's nice," I said as I paused for a moment to listen to the refrain. "You know what we should do? Let's make this our song," I exclaimed to Samantha.

Up until now, we didn't have an "our song." We both appreciated the music of the day, but it was high time we had a nice little love song we could call our own. She agreed, and we decided to make it our own from there on out.

Smiling warmly, I then told Samantha, "I love you on purpose."

She looked at me a bit inquisitively. "What do you mean?" she said.

"Well, if you do decide to do something on purpose, you don't do it because you're forced to, or because it's a habit, or because you're just going through the motions of obligation," I told her. "You do it because of deliberate intent. I want you to know that I love you because I *choose* to. Because you're valuable to me and I *want* to purposefully love you. 'Not out of selfish ambition or vain conceit,'" as I quoted a verse from the Bible. "So long as you and I keep dating—and I sure hope it goes on forever—I will always *choose* to love you on purpose and never take your love for granted."

She paused for a moment, letting my words permeate her mind and heart as she pondered them.

"I love you on purpose, too," she told me, smiling coyly and blushing beneath the lines of soot that covered her sweet face.

With that, I took a long chug from my soda bottle. As I locked eyes with hers, I was mesmerized by how much they seemed to twinkle and shine from the late afternoon rays of sun that streamed in from the open door on the far side of the rail car shed. "What?" she demurely and playfully asked me. She always got squirmy whenever I'd linger a bit too long and admire her beauty a mere moment longer than she deemed befitting. Or whenever I got in one of my sappy romantic moods like the one just now. Her shy, playful spirit, laced with a hint of self-doubt, was utterly enchanting. I was drawn to the subtle nuances of her behavior, the way she laughed, the way she blushed. Every moment shared with her was a treasure, a fleeting glimpse into a world of pure joy and connection of both her character as well as the connection we were continually building.

As my mother bid us adieu from across the bay and departed, Samantha and I reconvened with Mr. Smith back at the front of the engine. Break time was over. Mr. Smith said that with the longer days and warming weather, in his opinion, we would soon be able to paint. For a locomotive this big, as well as a coal tender, we estimated it would take at least thirty gallons of paint. He encouraged me to reach out to my brother at the hardware store to see if he could get us a deal on some paint at cost, which I did. To do so, though, I was fearful that he would start asking questions. And while I was sure he would agreeably keep our secret clandestine, I didn't want to expand our circle of insiders any wider than it already was. Plus, I figured the fewer people who knew of this undertaking now, the more they would be surprised later when we finished, which would be extra exciting.

We devised a red-herring plan where I would go in and ask Charles what the cost would be for thirty gallons of black matte paint for a project that I was helping Mr. Smith with at school, and to see if he could get it for us at cost. Technically, this little white lie wouldn't be too far out of hand, since it was through Mr. Smith's history class at school anyhow where I first learned of the story of the *Tullahoma*. Charles would deliver it to the school and set it on the loading dock in the back, and as soon as he left, Mr. Smith and I would quickly load it in the back of his pickup to be driven over to the machine shed.

Not only did Charles agree to offer us a great price, but he also offered it to us at cost as a way of supporting the school. In addition, Charles said that another customer had ordered five gallons too many of solid red and white paint to repaint his barn, which was going to get thrown out. It was ours if we wanted it. Another stroke of luck! We had planned to paint the engine and coal tender completely black and then offset the name *Tullahoma* on each side, along with the cowcatcher and a few other decorative flairs, in a different color anyhow. We lucked out with accumulating more than enough paint for our project.

Chapter 21

On a Friday night in mid-May of 1962, Samantha and I were sitting in the porch swing at her house, swaying back and forth, nestled up in each other's arms. One of those late-spring evenings when the air hung heavy with the sweet scent of newly blossomed honeysuckle and fireflies began to twinkle in the gathering dusk.

"I want to get baptized," she blurted out, catching me a bit off guard. I had been so comfortable growing closer with Samantha, occasionally praying together or having a theological discussion from time to time, that I hadn't even considered that baptism was on her mind. I had been baptized as an infant, so I had just assumed she had as well, not realizing it was something that was missing from her life.

"Okay, then let's make it happen!" I said as I hugged her close and savored her words. Despite her family's lack of regular spiritual accountability, I was excited that Samantha eagerly wanted to take the next step in her personal faith.

We both dropped by the church the next day, as we figured that Pastor Robert would be there putting the finishing touches on his sermon and preparing for Sunday services the following morning. He invited us into his office, and he and Samantha talked over some basic New Testament precepts while I sat in a chair off to the side. He said he was free to perform her baptism that afternoon if she wanted to. She agreed, and Pastor Robert encouraged her to at least extend an invitation to her parents, explaining that they deserved the courtesy, even if their faith was lukewarm or they had no interest in attending.

Samantha went home to change into some older clothes, and I walked home to grab my bike and rejoin them at the creek where Pastor Robert had instructed us to meet in a short bit. Her family did come along with her, much to my delight. As the pastor read a few verses out of the Bible and had Samantha repeat a believer's response after him, he then passed his Bible to me on the shore. I set it safely on the dry bank and watched as he dipped her below the current of that cold late-spring water.

As soon as she came up, gasping from the shock of the cold water, I started clapping and whooping and hollering with excitement, and her parents and little sister joined in. I noticed that Samantha was wearing the silver heart locket I had given her for Christmas. Tears of joy welled up in my eyes. It felt as though, by wearing that piece of jewelry on that particular Saturday afternoon, she had taken a part of me under the current with her. Samantha didn't just take the plunge alone; she was, in a way, inviting me to share in her journey as well. Telling me that we were in this together. Our lives were growing more intertwined. Even more so, the knowledge that her soul was strengthened that day filled me with overwhelming joy.

Sentimentality chokes me up every time and always finds a way to tug at my heartstrings. In that moment, I completely disregarded getting my shoes wet as I stepped off the bank and onto a gravel bar in the shallow water below while Pastor Robert was helping Samantha back to shore. I gave her a huge hug with reckless abandon for how wet she was and the fact that I would get soaked, something I hadn't planned on but by no means was of concern at the moment. This girl meant so much to me, and I was so proud of her courage and growth in her prayer walk that I wanted to hug her so tight. I *needed* to hug her tight. As we tightly embraced while standing on a shallow gravel bar in the middle of the stream, I told her how proud I was of her. Once again, we were growing closer—not merely in the physical sense, but even greater in the spiritual sense.

As we stepped back onto the bank, I glanced at her father, who had a slight smile on his face. I appreciated his subtle nod of approval in that smile, that he was not only happy for his daughter but proud that I had helped Samantha to grow into her faith, even if it was something he wasn't fully ready to personally embrace himself. Seeds had been planted in that moment, though, and I said a silent *thank you* in my heart that the Lord was working in Mr. Jensen's heart as well, perhaps toward the idea of one day stepping out courageously in his own faith walk and as an example to his wife and Kathryn.

Kathryn handed Samantha a towel, and she dried off the best she could in her wet clothes, smiling and laughing. I was so excited that I got to experience this moment with my love and how the two of us had incorporated ourselves into each other's lives so tightly. So richly. I could not have been more proud of my gal. Mr. Jensen then invited both Pastor Robert and me over for a backyard barbecue and mulligan stew that evening to celebrate, and I eagerly accepted. I was thankful that he recognized the importance of this moment and the need for celebration, and I couldn't wait for whatever new adventures the Lord next placed before the two of us.

Chapter 22

School was out for the summer in late May, and by early June we committed several days to painting every component of the engine. Although I enjoyed high school for the most part, summer allowed me the freedom to pick up odd jobs around town in addition to my regular paper route to make a little extra money. I'd often pass out fliers to mow lawns when townspeople were on vacation, help my brother at the hardware and feed store unload trucks whenever the new inventory deliveries arrived, and sometimes various farmers would call upon me for an extra hand for the day to mend fences, muck corrals or pig pens, and stack bales of hay.

I particularly liked these agricultural jobs because the farmer would usually pick me up right after I was done with my paper route. For a townsperson, it almost seemed like a mini working vacation to venture into the countryside. Often, there were horses, donkeys, or other farmyard critters to admire, and I particularly liked scratching the soft fur just inside their ears or the velvet of their noses. Lunch was particularly exciting, at which time we would usually take a break from our task at hand, and the farm wife would typically prepare an extensive spread of food, eager to show off her cooking skills to a visitor. The odd jobs I would often take were flexible, but after all, I still had a girlfriend I wanted to impress and needed the money in order to take her out once in a while. It was also important to me that her father viewed me as a diligent and hard worker, and I tried to squirrel away some savings for whatever awaited me post-high school, be it college or whatever other path I found.

As the summer progressed and we shifted our focus to painting the locomotive, Mr. Smith, with his limp and bone spurs, primarily worked at ground level, using a small stool to reach a few slightly elevated areas. We read that mixing the paint with oil and graphite would help preserve the life of the engine, so Mr. Smith prepared the mixture, which stunk to the high heavens. I clamored all around the cab, smokestack, and roof to paint. Samantha found her niche and skill provided most proficiently at painting the intricate and finer details with a smaller brush. Her slender arms were also quite adept at painting the hard-to-reach places Mr. Smith and I couldn't wriggle into.

By the third ten-hour day, the three of us had finished painting the entire engine, and it looked like something out of a haunted amusement ride. No markings or details, just black, as if it were a hearse in the ghostly dead of night. We then used the red and white paint that my brother had given to us and traced several decorative trim lines on the engine, smokestack, and coal tender car to offset it and give it a little color and design. All of the photos we had to rely on from the 1800s were in black and white, so we took the artistic liberty of adding color where we felt it looked the best.

In the shop, we found several sheet metal stencils and used them to carefully line T U L L A H O M A and the engine's original number, "No. 5," below the engineer's window on both sides. The engine looked absolutely beautiful in spite of our several months of amateur hard work. Not nearly as perfect as when it had come off the assembly line in 1861, but between my father's earlier restoration efforts and our rehab work now, it looked sleek, sharp, and ready for business. We all stood back to admire the details, shapes, and lines that made up this magnificent machine.

Running well ahead of schedule, we felt as though we were in a place to relax our pace a bit. After all, the town centennial wasn't for another year. Mr. Smith and I would have to do some extensive study in steam locomotive operation since actually firing up the engine was completely out of our wheelhouse—and God forbid, we start an unintentional fire or explosion. There would also be the logistics of coal, oil, and water to ensure we had at our disposal all that the locomotive needed to be safely powered alive. With school out for the summer, Mr. Smith left on an extended vacation to visit his relatives in Baltimore, and I resumed my various odd part-time summer jobs while Samantha helped her folks around their home, seeing each other from time to time as our schedules allowed.

Chapter 23

Now the Fourth of July in any small town is no small celebration, and Paxton certainly went all out to party for the nation's birthday as large as anywhere. The town council hosted a huge annual picnic in the square, complete with a horseshoe throwing competition, a pie walk, a patriotic bandstand in the gazebo, and a barbecue picnic complete with hot dogs and hamburgers. Wives and other women would usually donate side dishes to share with the town, eager to display a new recipe they had read of in *Ladies' Home Journal* or *Good Housekeeping* and wanted to try out. Nobody went away hungry, that much was certain. At dusk, the local VFW hosted a grand fireworks display, accompanied by the thunderous roar of several cannons, which echoed through the valley and seemed to cause even the leaves of the trees in the park to vibrate and tremble under the intense booms. It was a grand spectacle to experience, and one that everybody from town excitedly raved about for weeks, both leading up to and afterward.

A cool, quiet stillness hung in the air as the July 4th morning dawned. Prior to the evening's festivities, Samantha and I borrowed her dad's Buick to drive to the Coldwater Mill, a relic of a bygone era when the old grist mill once hummed with activity. Located along Coldwater Creek ten miles outside of town, the mill sat downriver from the same stream that flowed out from the Paxton reservoir. Long since abandoned, the giant waterwheel, drive shaft, and gears were still intact. The waterwheel shaft had long since rusted and ceased turning, so kids would often climb out onto the wheel itself and sit in the buckets overlooking the river to hang out, almost like sitting atop a motionless Ferris wheel of sorts.

It reminded me a bit of the ice house in *Bye Bye Birdie,* and was a place where kids would often go to party. The abandoned mill was way too wild a place on Friday and Saturday nights for me, with lots of heavy drinking, smoking, and drugs going on. Occasionally, you'd hear of fistfights breaking out over some silly squabble, like somebody making eyes at the wrong girl or insulting the wrong narcissistic drunk guy's car—as if it were a literal extension of himself. Plus, the mill was technically private property, though no one seemed to know whose land lay claim to it anymore. Legend was that moonshine bootleggers would still occasionally stop by as a well known off-the-beaten-path rustic meeting point to exchange their contraband with buyers.

On this Fourth of July morning, though, all was quiet. Parking our car a short distance away and hiking in, we noticed that several beer bottles littered the otherwise dusty floors, sagging with age and slow rot from the humid Alabama summertime heat as it slowly crumbled away. We explored the building, I not having been there in a long time and Samantha seeing it for her first time. Knowing her penchant for adventure and always being up for discovering something new, I wanted to take her somewhere fresh and exciting. Climbing up the rickety stairs and first exploring the attic, we peered out of the two small windows on either side of the rafters. With the glass panes long since broken out—or likely shot out—we realized our height above ground level in the precipice was almost three stories above the creek.

Someone had tied a huge rope onto one of the highest rafters of the top floor, and you could actually climb down a shaft to the main level three platforms below. What's a boyfriend for if not someone to challenge you to a little friendly competition, so I dared Samantha to climb down the rope just one level onto the next platform below.

Chickening out, she countered with, "Why don't you climb down the rope and I'll take the stairs, and we will see who gets there first!" a challenge I quickly accepted. As I twisted my legs and feet around the rope like a pretzel and yelled "Go," I mostly slid the twelve feet or so to the third story, trying to avoid rope burn on my hands as she raced down a flight of wobbly old wooden stairs to meet me below.

"I think it was a draw; better luck next time!" she said, laughing as she swatted me on the butt while I untwisted myself from the rope and regained my footing on the landing.

We then walked down another level to check out the big waterwheel, sort of the highlight of the mill. Carefully climbing first out onto the waterwheel from a small window at its apex, I reached a hand back for a hesitant Samantha to follow. She wasn't as sure about this as I was, but I reassured her that the waterwheel's hub had long since rusted with age and had solidly molded itself in place. She carefully took my hand and walked out onto the first paddle. We stepped over a couple more until we found one that was almost level at a ninety-degree angle, where we both sat down. Our feet dangled freely over the edge as we watched the water flow beautifully over the low-head dam just upstream from the mill.

The dam had been built a century before as a way to channel the flow of the creek in order to turn the wheel, through a series of cogs and rods that would grind cornmeal into a fine powder for bread making and other purposes. It was beautiful and relaxing as we gazed out over the water and onto the distant meadow of summer timothy grass and heather on the far side of the stream. Samantha leaned in to kiss me while in this peaceful setting of serenity and bliss, and I cupped her beautiful face with my right hand as I leaned in to meet her halfway. She smelled as sweet and fresh as the morning dew itself, and my hand nestled in to feel the warmth and softness of her hair at the base of her neck along her nape.

After a few moments of passionate kissing, she leaned back shyly and smiled but quickly changed the subject in classic shy Samantha fashion.

"What do you think you're going to do next year after we graduate from high school?" she asked me.

It was a fair question. We had been dating for nine months. Nine months of shared laughter, deep thoughts, and a growing tenderness I couldn't deny. I owed her an honest answer, a glimpse into the future that both thrilled and terrified me. She was looking for something more, I knew it. A promise and direction for us. We had built something special dating during our junior year, something precious. We'd weathered storms together, celebrated small victories, and learned to navigate the intricate dance of our growing connection. I cared for her deeply, profoundly, and a soft voice in the back of my head whispered that she might be the one. Thoughts of my future—both with Samantha as well as my own career path after high school—exhilarated yet overwhelmed me.

Back then, many high school sweethearts ended up married. I loved her without reservation, but I knew I needed to figure out my life path. I had considered joining the Air National Guard—voluntarily, of course—not through a forced military draft like my father. I knew way too many men who had suffered through the Great War. Honorable men. Patriotic men. Men who had been physically and mentally changed by the scars of the terrible war. The Korean War had ended just a few years prior, and now the country was sending young men off to fight a new campaign—in Vietnam—once again a half a world away. I would absolutely answer the call to defend my country and all that I held dear. But did I particularly want to volunteer to run off to battle and leave the one girl behind that I truly loved, and who loved me in return? The thought of being gone for months, or even years, filled me with dread. Would she wait for me? Or would the distance and the uncertainty drive us apart? The insecurity gnawed at me.

I truly enjoyed learning, and my academic achievements were always very strong. College highly appealed to me, and I wanted to attend a university to become a history teacher like my role model, Mr. Smith. But that took money that I just didn't have, and I wondered if I should take out a loan and go into debt to pay for it. Our windfall of gaining ownership of the abandoned rail yard would likely give me a financial boost, but I wasn't certain if it was enough.

Samantha had previously expressed an interest in going to college too, but she also told me long term she'd be plenty happy being a homemaker and having a couple of kids. It would sure be great if we could go to the same college, though, but I knew her family's financial situation was much stronger than my mother's.

Samantha expressed that this fall she was going to apply to Belmont College in Nashville. Her father and mother had met there when they were in college, and her daddy said he would pay for her degree if she selected the same alma mater as him. I had always dreamed of visiting Nashville after reading books about its rich history, great food, and lively country western music scene. After we talked things over atop the waterwheel, I concluded that this fall I would apply to Belmont as well. I had saved almost enough money for one year and hopefully could obtain a few scholarships to pay for the rest. Plus, I couldn't fathom spending time apart from my beloved.

Chapter 24

Just then, we heard the distant unmistakable noise of a couple of dirt bikes coming up the narrow trail that ran along the creek that halted our conversation. The rumble of the engines pierced the stillness of the morning. And they were inbound fast. We spotted the plume of dust before we saw the bikes themselves as they got closer, and I couldn't believe my eyes when I saw none other than Boone and Oliver riding them. *Where did those two idiots get motorcycles?* I thought to myself in disgust. *Probably stolen.*

Samantha started to panic. I reassured her not to worry; they had come in from the north and not from where we had parked her dad's car along the west, so they probably didn't even know we were here. "Let's just sit still and be silent and see what they're going to do," I told her. "If we stay quiet, they might not even know we are here and quickly pass on through," I said optimistically, reassuring her as much as I was actually reassuring myself.

As they parked their dirt bikes just out of eyesight, we could hear their voices as they came into the mill, cussing and joking and carrying on as hoodlums do. I slowly and quietly climbed from our perch midway down the waterwheel back up to the top level so I could peek through the open window to hear and see better. Samantha cowered slightly below and behind me, and thankfully the noise from the low-head waterfall dampened any noise we made by shifting around on the waterwheel.

From the window, and down through the slightest gap in the floor as I peered from our perch, I could see Boone pull what looked like a couple of marijuana cigarettes out of his pocket, and the two sat down on a couple of old wooden spools, lighting up their weed. We could faintly hear them laughing and joking about how hard they planned to party and drink all Fourth of July weekend long. As they stumbled and slurred their speech, it seemed as though this wasn't their first hit of the day. I silently lifted my index finger to my lips to reassure Samantha to be quiet and still. It still made sense that our best course of action was just to bide our time as they got high, and then hopefully they'd ride off again. That way we wouldn't have to involve ourselves with interacting with the two hot-headed drunk stoners.

Unfortunately, though, I was mistaken in my decision of peacefully waiting it out—disaster was looming and a powder keg was about to explode. Finishing their tokes, Boone reached in his pocket and pulled out two more joints and Oliver pulled out a pack of lights. Always one to hoist his own petard, and being quite high at this point, Boone dropped the lit match onto the wooden threshing floor. There must have been whiskey spilled from a party the night before that permeated into the floorboards, because all at once the floor went up in a whoosh of flame. The two jug heads, not even initially realizing at first what had happened, began dancing and hopping like a couple of Indians in a rain dance as they tried to tamp it out. It was useless, though; years of chaff and dust that had settled between the old floorboards had provided enough tinder that the fire quickly spread down the rows of dry planks. Seeing they were in way over their heads and beyond toked at this point, the two panicked idiots then raced out of the mill and we could hear the sound of their motorcycles fire up as they quickly sped off.

Samantha grabbed my hand out of fear. My heart jumped and my mind raced as the adrenaline kicked in. Not only was this blaze rapidly becoming out of control, but I quickly calculated that we probably wouldn't have enough time to scamper back into the mill from our perch on the waterwheel and dash through the flames to the other side before they would consume us. We needed to think fast, though, because this place was quickly becoming engulfed by smoke and fire.

"Quick!" I told Samantha. "Let's climb back down the waterwheel as far as we can. Once we get back to that ninety-degree plank where we were sitting moments earlier, we have to jump!"

"No way!" she said. "I'm not dying on the rocks below!"

"The water had to be deep enough, at least as deep as the wheel's arc below the surface," I exclaimed. Fueled by recent summer rains, the stream surged with a strong current.

There was no time to hesitate. "We have to jump, and we have to jump *now!*" I urgently yelled to her.

Grabbing ahold of her hand and reassuring her once more, I said, "We do this on 'three.' Both of us together. Okay?"

I needed to know she was fully committed to jumping with me. It was my responsibility as her boyfriend to protect her at all costs, and I couldn't bear to live with myself had I jumped and she hesitated and stayed up on the waterwheel, electing to try and find a path out through the building, which was completely out of the question at this point.

"Umm… Okay," she said, wavering and less than assuredly. But as the flames grew bigger and we could feel the heat begin to singe our faces, her commitment to jump was solid enough. I told her once we jump, the plan is to then swim downstream to where we can circle back to the shore.

"Trust me. I've got you," I said to her, as calmly as my dry voice would allow me to utter in the frantic situation.

At that, it was *One, Two, Three. . .* As the smoke began to waft out of the small window at the top of the waterwheel, we stepped off the platform in unison. I grabbed her hand tighter than I ever had before to ensure there was no way she'd hesitate and back out, since there was no way that I was leaving her to face the raging inferno.

We both hit the water in a splash, and my hand slipped off Samantha's when we connected with the surface of the cold, slippery water. I looked around feverishly for a moment while I paddled in place. Left, then right, wiping the muddy creek water from my face. "Samantha!" I yelled. Just then, her head popped above the surface a few feet away. Taking a moment to catch our breath and ensuring we were both okay as we treaded water, we quickly doggy paddled to shore.

We climbed out of the water soaking wet and turned to look upstream. The mill was completely consumed in a great conflagration of flames and black smoke that extended upward to the heavens. Looking up to where the smoke pierced the otherwise cloudless, picturesque blue summertime sky, I figured the closest volunteer fire department would be here in fifteen minutes or less, and we surely didn't want to be caught as the only people anywhere close. It would look awfully suspicious, and we certainly didn't want to have to go through an intense questioning and interrogation session that was sure to follow. We needed to hightail it back to the car to get out of Dodge fast.

Opening the trunk, we found a couple of old shop towels in the back that would have to make do at spot-drying us off as best we could. We would have to strip down to our skivvies, or else we were going to get a bunch of stinky creek water all over her dad's nice car. Changing out of our wet clothes, and stuffing them in the trunk like we were Bonnie and Clyde who had just committed some bank heist and needed a speedy costume change, we quickly drove off and headed back to town.

As I pulled from the dirt lane onto the main highway north into town, I looked over at Samantha and started laughing. "Don't look at me!" she snapped back while trying to cover as much of her shivering self as she could with her hands, but I couldn't help it.

"We better just pray the cops don't pull us over right now because I don't think they'd believe our story if we told them!" I said to her in a nervous laugh. "Here I am, driving a car that's not mine, leaving the scene of an arson, both of us damp with creek water, and sitting in our underwear while the rest of our wet clothes are shoved in the trunk."

Heck, I'm not even sure if I would believe the story myself if I had repeated it. It was so outlandish and wild.

I paid particular attention to the speed limit signs, and we took the back roads into Paxton. As we neared the edge of town, a couple of fire trucks passed us heading in the direction from whence we came, lights flashing and sirens wailing as they trailed in the distance. We both just looked at each other and playfully gritted our teeth as we shrugged our shoulders uncomfortably and pressed on toward town.

We needed a place to change clothes and hide for a few hours while our clothes dried. I knew that, with it being a holiday, neither my place nor Charles' house was safe for us to slip into, as everyone was off work and likely hanging near home. Samantha's family would be at their place, so that wasn't safe either. As innocent as we were, simply victims of being in the wrong place at the wrong time, I didn't want to have to answer a bunch of invasive questions. Especially with both of us in our underwear in the conservative Bible Belt—it didn't exactly look pure and innocent—even if it truly was. So, I went to the only place I could think of that was private: the rail car repair building. Even that would take some careful navigating, pulling into it and opening the gate without anyone spotting us.

As I pulled up to the perimeter fence, we looked both ways to make sure no other cars were coming by. Not hearing any approaching traffic and not seeing any pedestrians, I made a mad dash from the car to the gate, scrambling to unlock it in my underwear before anyone spotted us. We quickly drove on through the gate and repeated the same covert procedure to open the door to the shop itself, quickly flinging open the arched doors before I raced back to the car. Driving the car inside the large entrance alongside the edge of the rails, I ran back to the door to shut us inside. Finally, we could breathe a sigh of relief.

Oh my gosh, what in the heck just happened! I thought to myself, finally able to decompress and take stock of everything that had happened. Samantha was understandably reluctant to step out of the car in her state of minimal dress, but I remembered just then that we both had our work coveralls hanging up on the wall, along with a couple of old t-shirts. Of course, they were filthy, but they would have to suffice. I went and got my overalls and quickly slipped them on, and brought Samantha hers, along with a dry t-shirt.

"Go into the office and change, and I'll wait here," I told her.

"Okay, but you have to turn around while I run over to the office, no peeking!" she commanded me.

"Fine, fair enough," I said, handing her the dry overalls and t-shirt through the car window. She quickly bounded off to the office while I stared toward the far wall. At the last second, right before she stepped into the office, though, I turned around to glance and caught the shape of her cute little bottom through her underwear in the distance as she turned the corner and went into the office. *Boys will be boys—I'm a guy and can't help it!* I thought as I giggled to myself before gathering up all of our wet clothes from the trunk and hanging them on a couple of sapling branches outside to air-dry in the hot July sun.

After we were both temporarily in our work overalls and awaiting our other clothes to dry, we climbed up on the platform deck of the locomotive cab and sat down on the floor of the platform, dangling our legs over the edge between the back of the locomotive and the coal tender. It was eerily reminiscent of the position we had been sitting in together on the edge of the waterwheel at the mill just forty-five minutes earlier, legs hanging over the side.

"So what are your future *family* plans?" Samantha asked without missing a beat, quickly reverting to our prior conversation encompassing our future and diverting the conversation from any awkwardness of just seeing each other in our underwear a few moments earlier. I could tell that she wasn't done with our previous hour's discussion about long-term thoughts, as she narrowed the conversation to more direct relational and intimate family planning now rather than broader career or education aspirations. She wasn't just asking me about my personal future, but positing more as to how I had thought of her and me together when I considered my future—how she factored into my life and any future children I might want.

"Well, I've always thought two would be a good number of kids," I started. Considering that I grew up in a home with just my brother and me, and recollecting how the financial strain was tough on my mother at times, I knew that I never wanted to feel unable to adequately provide for my family, whether it be with quality time or with finances.

Knowing Samantha and Kathryn also came from a two-sibling family, I continued, "I've always thought that I'd rather concentrate my time and love on just two kids rather than ever feel like it was spread too thin among a large number of children."

She just sort of sat there, mulling it over, chewing on every word I had answered. Feeling the need to affirm my love for her and put her mind at ease as well as inject a little humor to lighten the conversation, I continued, "You have a huge heart, and I think when you become a mother someday, you will make the best possible mom. But of course, we have to get through high school first. Heck, first we need to keep each other out of jail for arson!" I said jokingly.

Without uttering a word, she thunked me on the shoulder for making light of what had just happened and the brevity of our now-serious situation. But then she placed her head on my shoulder and nuzzled up to me. And I knew she was happy.

We then puttered around the shop for a bit, biding our time until our clothes dried. We played a makeshift game of ring toss with a metal band from a fifty-five-gallon oil barrel and a makeshift rail spike we found laying around the shop. It was now past lunchtime and I was starving. I knew after our clothes dried, I needed to get Samantha back home so we could both freshen up before the town picnic—and to return the borrowed car of her dad's. People would start to assemble downtown for the evening's festivities in a few hours, and I knew I'd get to see her again soon enough. Checking our clothes and sufficing them to be dry enough, we each got changed back into our regular clothes and I ran her home.

After dropping Samantha and her dad's car off and beginning the walk back home, my thoughts kept reverting to what Boone and Oliver had done by burning down the mill. Should I go to the police? Wait and see what the climate of the gossip is at the Independence Day picnic tonight—as the old mill fire would certainly be the talk of the town? *Or just take the secret to the grave?* I decided just to take a wait-and-see approach. Would anything truly be done as a result of Boone and Oliver getting arrested? Probably not. And if they did get tossed in jail, it would mean there would be nobody else to work with their daddy on the cotton plantation, so he'd either be in a world of hurt financially and possibly lose the farm, or drink himself to death—a line to which he already tiptoed way too closely. Although I loved the old mill and it was fun to explore and reminisce over its history, it was a tinderbox and a death trap and a source for questionable behavior. So it probably wouldn't be the worst thing that it was now gone, I figured.

Chapter 25

Reconvening at the city park later that evening at 7:00 p.m., the setting was a pure festivity. The smells of the VFW barbecue filled the air as people gathered and laughed, and kids ran around playing tag and blowing bubbles. American flags were hung all over, and it was great to see crisp fifty-star flags since Hawaii had recently been admitted as a state. I spotted Mr. Jensen talking with several men that I recognized as fellow coal miners who lived in town. Samantha, her mother, and sister were already laying out a blanket on the grass. Seeing my mother and me walk up, Samantha and her mom invited us to sit next to them to watch the fireworks. We quickly set our blanket and drinks down, and before we got in line for our picnic dinner, I invited Samantha and Kathryn to light some sparklers that I had brought along.

As we were laughing and having a splendid time waving our sparklers in the dusk sky, an old WWII P-51 Mustang someone must have purchased after the war as government surplus did a couple of low passes overhead. Everybody looked up and cheered loudly as the plane did loops and spins, and we were filled with patriotic pride in our community and the heritage of what our nation represented.

It also made me reflect upon the dichotomy of disunity and how the Old South fought long and hard to preserve its Southern traditions and way of life during the Civil War. The nation was deeply divided. Yet WWII had a way of uniting the country in a way that was unparalleled since perhaps the

Revolutionary War, by bringing people together. Wars have a way of doing that: some cause passionate resistance and hatred of the other side, with a climate of poignant divisiveness from within. But when persevering to defeat a common enemy or threat from the outside, wars can instill incredible unity and national pride.

I thought even more intently of the locomotive we had been restoring, a Southern emblem that fell victim to the North as Federal troops sought to disable the Confederacy. If we were successful in bringing the locomotive back to life, would it bring back pain and divisiveness, or instill wholeness in the town? Could it serve as a memorial of sorts, an archaeological time machine and museum piece that could teach history for what it was during the time period it had taken place? Or would it dredge up long-suppressed feelings of Confederate separation, anger, and pain?

As my mind was adrift, I remembered Boone and Oliver —whom I just realized while scanning the crowd were nowhere to be found. *I suppose they're laying low after what they did earlier today,* I thought. Although you'd think the best approach would probably be to blend in with the crowd as a way of laying low, even if it meant observing from the periphery, it seemed more suspicious to be completely absent from the town's biggest celebration of the year. Even though they showed up to church some Sundays and put their butts in a pew along with the rest of us, listening to the same sermons of personal growth, kindness, compassion, and love, they never seemed to *get it.* They went through the motions of life, maintaining their trouble-making persona without actually having a deeper heart change in the end.

I thought back to my mother's statement that my father always said, "Whenever you feel like criticizing anyone, just remember that all the people in this world haven't had the advantages that you've had." How do you bridge the gap of anger and bitterness to one of community and hope? It isn't an easy feat, something only the Lord could change in a person's heart, I surmised. Or perhaps a change He could enact through the intervention of another. My cynicism began to creep into my thoughts again, though, as I thought of the mill going up in smoke. I certainly didn't see myself as the person to create a turnaround in them.

I redirected my thoughts back to the moment at hand, though. As the fireworks exploded in a brilliance of color overhead, I reached my hand over to touch Samantha's as we both reclined on a blanket to watch the beautiful display. It made me proud to live in a country where our freedom and safety were assured, thanks to men like my father who had given so dearly over the centuries to ensure the enduring spirit of lasting patriotism on Independence Day.

Chapter 26

Late August 1962 embodied the fleeting dog days of summer—those languid afternoons where the sun lingers stubbornly, and a heavy humidity clings to the first shadows of dusk. The earth seemed to hold its breath, anticipating the crisp arrival of a cooler fall soon to come.

Samantha and I had both completed our applications for Belmont College and mailed them away. She made me kiss her envelope for good luck, and she did the same for mine. It was a silly little superstition, but I let her have it, as I thought how amazing it would be to both end up at the same school. If it worked, it worked, and I was willing to give anything a try.

Samantha completely captivated me with her enthusiasm for never saying no to an adventure, whether it was going fishing, exploring the abandoned mill, attending church with me for the first time, riding our bikes down a new path—or restoring an old forgotten locomotive that nobody even knew we had. Going away to Belmont and attending college together would just be one more adventure to add to the books. That is, if I could still actually figure out a way to pay for it.

Feeling a bit sentimental one evening after dinner, I walked over to the repair shop by myself. All was quiet and serene. The shop was already starting to get dark under the setting sun, but long shadows from the transom windows above set the tone for a reflective moment of thoughtful meditation and yearning of a serious future with Samantha. I sat down at the desk in the office, and, flipping on the desk lamp, I pulled out a faded blank piece of acetone-age paper from within a drawer. With the urge of sentimentality and expressing my feelings, I began to pen a heartfelt poem for Samantha:

The Only Thing You Hooked (Was Me)

As soon as school was out, we'd meet up at the lake
Hoping to reel in whatever swam by
Get all the sunburn we could take
And fish 'till fireflies filled the sky
We'd dream of our future plans,
and all that could ever be,
But your line was empty, the only thing you hooked was
me
We'd climb the hickory tree so high
Ride bikes to our secret spot in the woods
Lay on a blanket underneath the stars
And talk of making it big in Hollywood
We'd dream of our future plans,
and all that could ever be,
But your line was empty, the only thing you hooked was
me
As we rode horses on that country farm
Your auburn hair tossed by the breeze above
I'd catch you smile at my goofy charm
In those hills I found my first love
We'd dream of our future plans,
and all that could ever be,

But your line was empty, the only thing you hooked was
me
Soon the days will turn crisp and cold
Grey skies will give way to snow
Seasons wedge time and space between us
But there's one thing I must know
Can we do it again next summer, can I have your
guarantee?
Of all the fish in the sea, the only one you hooked was
me.

The poem tucked safely in my pocket, I savored the anticipation of sharing it with her at precisely the right moment. I knew Samantha's feelings mirrored mine, a quiet certainty that warmed me as I reflected on a past moment when she said that my genuine tenderness towards her was one of my sweetest qualities. There existed this yearning within me, a need to express the depth of my emotions as a young man often must to his love, to capture her renewed confirmation and sincere pledge in return.

Our shared adventure with the locomotive had forged an unbreakable connection. While I was initially hesitant that Samantha would share my same alacrity for this project, her initial apprehension quickly gave way to vibrant enthusiasm. We challenged each other, supported each other, and had fun doing so as we shared an effortless chemistry. We made a pretty great team, and if the past year was any indication of what our future could be, I'd say we had the potential for an exciting future ahead.

Chapter 27

As the sweltering summer turned to the cool embrace of autumn, the start of my senior year loomed closer. One particular late-summer's evening held a cherished memory from my adolescence.

Paxton, though a significant stop for coal trains along the Alabama & Tennessee Railroad system, was merely a "whistle stop" – a brief pause for passenger and cargo exchanges as it chugged between Huntsville, Scottsboro, Rome, Georgia, and points beyond. Rolling stock, and an occasional locomotive, were occasionally broken off from the rest of the train and shuttled into the repair yard for maintenance before later rejoining other trains in future service. Yet Paxton was never a major hub. The railroad itself tried to minimize expenses where it could, taking advantage of the region's particularly low labor and living costs by operating the repair shop. However, trains were at no time provisioned with operational necessities in Paxton.

At the far back of the rail yard stood a water tower, and I had heard stories that it was primarily on-site to service the mechanical needs of the rail car facility. However, it could also be used to supply water for passing steam trains should they run low and have unexpected needs.

As a child, I viewed this rusty giant with a mischievous eye. I would often pluck cherry tomatoes from our garden, much to my mother's chagrin, and use them as ammunition in my slingshot as I aimed for the ampersand in the faded "A & T" logo that adorned the side of the tower. The satisfying *ping* of a bullseye was usually achieved with a quarter-sized green tomato, since the ground around my house contained more clay loam than rocks, and I quickly discovered that splattered tomatoes provided a gratification unparalleled for a middle school boy. Although one childhood memory vividly recalls a sharp stem still attached to a particular tomato slicing the back of my hand between my left thumb and pointer, requiring four stitches at the outpatient clinic in town – a bit of karma that came back to bite me for harvesting ammunition from the family vegetable garden.

Now, years later, with full access to the once-forbidden rail yard, I yearned to climb atop the water tower. Not in the sense that I wanted to vandalize the relic and spray-paint the name of my beloved on the side of it, but purely for the sake of adventure and curiosity of exploring it. An Everest to conquer as it summoned my wonder. In the early 1950s, when I was still a youngster, a small tornado had torn off the conical top, leaving only the cylindrical kettle frame. Yet the tower still stood sentinel as a local landmark, visible from much of the town.

One late August evening, Samantha and I, recognizing the advantage of the axiom "it is better to seek forgiveness than ask for permission" from either of our parents, embarked on our mission to tackle the iron-corroded behemoth. As the sun dipped just below the horizon, crepuscular light gave way, providing the perfect cover of semi-darkness to cloak our ascent. Samantha, in jeans and a red plaid-checked shirt, adorned with a bandanna as a hair covering, was as eager as I. We approached the tower, the iron ladder welded onto one of the four legs beckoning us to climb.

As I grabbed hold of the rails that flanked the iron ladder, I looked over at Samantha in an *are we really doing this?* pose. It was met with an *if you're in, I'm in* glance.

"No risk, no story," I said smiling to Samantha confidently before glancing upward at the path of our ascent.

I took the lead as I placed a foot on the first rail and began climbing upward, coaxing Samantha to not look down and to just focus above as she climbed just behind me—a reassurance I needed as much for myself as I relayed to her—as we quickly climbed the length of the multi-story leg to limit our exposure of being spotted by any passersby.

Reaching the platform that encompassed the kettle and with leg muscles aching from the climb, I tested the railing for stability with my brown iron-oxide-stained hands, and it seemed solid despite many decades of age. Below and to the south, we looked out over the town, its lights twinkling. It was easy to discern the high school stadium by its bright mercury vapor lighting as the school football team took advantage of cooler evening temperatures to conduct preseason practices.

As we walked around the platform to the north side, it was more shrouded in darkness from the forest that lay beyond. Punctuated by a chorus of tree frogs that had begun to wake up for the night, the shadowy canopy of the north woods offered a stark contrast to the urban glow of the town to the south.

I challenged Samantha to climb with me the rest of the way up the cylindrical kettle to see what was inside and she readily accepted. This feat was a bit more daunting, and I felt my fingers and arms tingle from the knowledge that the only thing between us and sudden death was a slip of our hands or feet from the rusty iron ladder rungs. As I peered over the top of the tower at its apex, I could see bent metal from where a small tornado had torn off the top of the water tower a decade prior. The dizzying effects of being up so high, with not so much as a rope to provide a sense of security, left me slightly vertiginous.

There still existed old maintenance steps inside the empty tower, which felt surprisingly sturdy as I swung a leg over the side of the top ledge and climbed down inside the dry bowl. Stepping onto the interior bottom, I reached up to guide Samantha as she carefully descended the remaining rungs. The interior of the tower, with its tapered slanted floor beneath, felt strangely surreal. We now stood twenty feet below the top of the wall, gazing upward at the deepening star-strewn twilight sky.

Suddenly, Samantha pushed me against the iron wall, her lips meeting mine in a playful, unexpected kiss as she pinned me to the wall. I was caught off guard but captivated by the scent of her perfume as she pressed her body closer, her hands playfully exploring my jeans pockets while I cradled her head in my hands. Our shared conquest of the tower seemed to have emboldened her, and it became clear to me that this experience had given her a newfound confidence —a seductive allure that was irresistible to postpone or defer. I was powerless to resist her advances, captivated by her intoxicating feminine beauty and charm. The secluded space within the tower offered an unexpected opportunity for intimacy, a level of closeness we could not particularly achieve elsewhere in our lives outside its walls. A particular rush of excitement pervaded the moment as we embraced high above the town, yet invisible to anyone outside of these iron walls.

I yielded to her embrace, relishing the feeling of the weight of her tender frame as we slinked to the floor of the tower, which formed a gentle slope as it beveled towards the standpipe below. My hands explored her slender hips and hourglass figure as our lips met again, and I found myself wanting more. I craved more of Samantha, in every sense of the word, desiring more bare skin contact and a deeper physical connection.

Yet despite our passionate intensity and lustful curiosity, a sense of shared understanding prevailed. We both recognized the virtue of restraint, tough as it was. As the fire of our hunger for intimacy subsided slightly, we held each other close and snuggled on the tapered base of the tower, the lingering warmth of the moment a testament to our physical connection. Our elevated heartbeats gradually lessened, replaced by a gentle sense of coziness and peace. Soon, however, we knew we needed to climb back down before pitch darkness set in, though neither of us wanted to relinquish this moment of contentment and bliss. Romance born from our shared penchant for adventure was quickly becoming a frequent bond that tied us together ever tighter.

Chapter 28

On a particularly pleasant early September weekend, I recalled the generous offer from a family whose farm I had assisted with mucking their pig pens earlier that summer—an invitation to ride their horses at my leisure. They had remembered my fondness for their horses from my time working at the farm, and when they informed me they were in need of someone to feed their barnyard livestock while away from the farm one weekend, I jumped at the opportunity. In the spirit of bartering, I offered my assistance for free in exchange for allowing the use of a couple of their horses to take a trail ride, a simple arrangement that would afford me the perfect occasion to share another exciting adventure with Samantha. They happily agreed.

As Samantha got out of her dad's Buick and walked up to our front porch, I was already sitting on the front steps awaiting her arrival. I could hardly believe my eyes; she was dressed in a plaid western shirt, cowboy hat, brown leather cowboy boots, and tight boot-cut jeans that highlighted her long, slender legs and revealed perfect curves in all of the right places. In the front of her jeans, she wore a shiny belt buckle that made the entire ensemble look official.

"Wow, you definitely dressed the part. You look great!" I told her.

I wasn't sure how much experience Samantha had with horses. She mentioned riding "a few" times in the past, although I wasn't certain of her level of comfort. While I was no expert myself, I had picked up the basics of horsemanship through various summer jobs on local farms throughout the years, and I hoped she'd catch on quickly. I certainly didn't want to spend the entire ride explaining every nuance, though I hoped she'd at least hold onto the reins tightly while trying.

Upon reaching the farm, Samantha's curiosity was immediately piqued by the farm animals. She wandered off to check out the goats and pigs, while a soft-looking black barn cat perched on the corral fence watched me intently as I prepared the horses for our ride—a tall, majestic brown quarter horse and a playful dappled paint. After gazing all googly-eyed at the smaller animals and talking to them in a silly voice, Samantha circled back to the barn, her eyes sparkling as she chattered on about the goats and domestic ducks. I just quietly listened and smiled. I then helped her onto the painted pony, and I adjusted the stirrups to fit her legs. Following suit, I mounted and dismounted my horse a couple of times until I found the perfect stirrup length for myself.

When we were both atop our horses and ready for our trail ride, I was just about to explain to Samantha how to hold the reins and to give her horse a gentle nudge to get it to walk, but in a flash, she hollered over to me, "Let's see what this guy can do!"

Before I could say anything, she kicked the sides of her horse and made a "click click" sound with her mouth and all at once was off in a flash! *Oh no,* I thought to myself, *here we are on a couple of borrowed horses. . . how will I explain to the owners if one runs off?! I thought their horses were supposed to be docile and broken? And even worse, how will Samantha dismount without getting hurt?!* But it only took a moment before I realized that Samantha was in complete control of the animal she was riding as a consummate professional—this certainly wasn't her first rodeo.

I watched Samantha head from the corral directly into the adjacent arena, which I assumed was just a larger pen to give the horses a little extra room to roam while still keeping them corralled close to the barn. In the arena space, though, three barrels were set up, and I watched while Samantha expertly guided her horse around the first two barrels. As she rounded the far one and began the turn for home, her horse grazed the edge of the metal Texaco oil drum and it began to tip. I watched as she confidently reached out her left hand to steady it from falling while grasping the reigns in her right. *Wow, that's an expert move!* I thought to myself.

In a dash of speed, with clumps of mud being flung skyward from the horse's hooves, she raced in a thunderous gallop back to where I nervously sat atop my horse as I impatiently waited for this little Annie Oakley trickster to be finished with her little rodeo spectacle. "Whoaaa!" she called out to her horse as she tugged back the reins, bringing it to a stop. "This guy can run pretty good!"

"What in the world?!" I called out to her. "Not only have you ridden more than just 'a few' times, but you're a little shyster! You had me fooled. . . are you a cowgirl or something? I thought your horse took off and I wouldn't find you again until the next county!"

Then again, I should have expected nothing less from Samantha; full of charisma and energy, she always kept me on my toes.

She laughed and asked me, "Didn't you see my belt buckle? I won it as the top barrel racer in my high school rodeo club last year back in Pennsylvania. When we first pulled into the farmyard, I noticed the arena and figured someone had been practicing and training these horses to run barrels, so I figured I'd see how good this one was. Not too shabby!"

I had noticed her buckle, but hadn't examined it closely enough to see what it said. I guess I had completely underestimated the garb that Samantha wore when she showed up, figuring she was just dressing the part as more of a city-slicker urban cowboy to try and impress me but without any actual skills to back it up. However, I was completely wrong, and it totally enthralled me that I witnessed such a spectacular display of riding skill and prowess. Still shaking my head in disbelief, I told her how I thought it was so neat how her old high school had an after-school club that taught horsemanship and equine skills, something we did not have here in Paxton. I envied what fun that club must have been.

The initial excitement subsided as we guided our horses out of the corral and settled into a more leisurely pace, enjoying the tranquility of the afternoon. We meandered through the meadows, the horses navigating the terrain with effortless grace. As we climbed steep ravines and splashed through a shallow brook, the horses' hooves sending up a cascade of water droplets, I was captivated by Samantha's adventurous spirit. She rode with a natural confidence, and the pure joy in her laugh and smile as she was completely in her element was infectious.

While I enjoyed sharing my knowledge of horsemanship, I quickly realized that I was learning as much from her in life than I could ever teach her. The prospect of sharing such experiences, of exploring the world together, filled me with a quiet sense of contentment as I tried to pause and capture each moment of bliss in my memory for eternity. A daisy in the meadow of my mind. As the sun dipped below the horizon, casting long shadows across the fields, we returned to the barn to feed and water the horses for the night.

Another day of adventure had come to a close, and my love for Samantha grew deeper with each passing moment. I remembered the poem I had written a couple of weeks ago that I had been carrying for just the right moment to give her. Pulling the piece of aged paper from my back pocket, I slipped it into her hand as she pulled into my driveway to drop me off for the night. "Don't open it until you've showered and are in your pajamas and all ready for bed," I instructed, wanting the mystery of my words to captivate her thoughts and build suspense until just before she turned in for the night.

The day had been filled with so much excitement and adventure, and I wasn't ready for it to end. I imagined her anticipation as she completed her evening routine to settle in for the night, my poem a prayer for her to dream upon. I hoped my note would ignite the warm embers of pleasure that filled our day, a reminder of the love and adventure that connect us even as the night momentarily divides us. A constant source of joy and inspiration, it was important to me that I often reminded Samantha how much she was on my mind. From dawn 'til dusk, and even in the quiet of the night, my thoughts were filled with Samantha—all that is pure and lovely. And my eagerness to see her at church the next morning filled me with a joy that would carry me through the night until we could meet once again.

Chapter 29

As school resumed, Mr. Smith returned from his summer in Massachusetts, regaling us with tales of his adventures. It was quite thrilling to live vicariously through stories of his summer sabbatical and the 35mm photographs he showed of the tall ships in Baltimore Harbor, baskets of Chesapeake Bay blue crabs, and exploring Fort McHenry, where the battle against the British inspired the *Star-Spangled Banner.*

With additional family members up in New England, Mr. Smith stated that he also spent some time in Boston. Flipping through more photos, I could see the wharves of the South Boston waterfront, the steeple of the Old North Church, and a side trip he took to Old Sturbridge Village—a colonial Quaker community complete with historic homes, a blacksmith shop, a cider mill, an 1800s schoolhouse, and more.

My fascination with history came alive as I poured over the captivating photographs of the intriguing historical sites Mr. Smith shared stories about. Places I dreamed of one day visiting. Coupled with my love for reading historical accounts in books and magazines and fueled by my strong interest in science and mechanics, Mr. Smith suggested that I consider a career as a history teacher or professor. I told him that I could warm up to that idea, although I liked the thought of ending up wherever Samantha did even more. Mr. Smith explained that I could complete my general studies courses in the first two years before I needed to commit to which degree to pursue, which eased my obsessive-compulsive mind a bit that typically thrived on predictability, order, and planning.

Mr. Smith went on to say that over the summer he had obtained copies of materials on the operation of the locomotive from a New England railway museum. We were both eager to pore over them. Self-educating ourselves would require quite a bit of discipline and understanding to gain the wisdom that a couple of amateurs needed, even for just the slightest chance of bringing the engine to life.

Given our complete lack of experience with railroad machinery and the absence of any local experts left in town to guide us, we would have to teach ourselves the basics. Starting with, how *do* these things even work?

Sure, we knew the elementary concept that water in the boiler is heated by the coal in the firebox, steam is produced, and that steam provides power to the pistons, the brakes, and the whistle. As we read deeper, the boiler water surrounds and insulates the firebox from becoming too hot, while the fire in turn heats the water. *Okay, that makes sense. Sort of a symbiotic relationship of sorts.* Steam pressure is monitored on one of those fancy gauges in the cab. If the water level becomes too high, the amount of steam produced fails, allowing little efficiency in moving the engine. If the steam pressure becomes too high or hot, damage can occur— possibly even an explosion. *Yikes!*

We needed to be on our game, and it would take a team effort to carefully prepare everything. After all, we were working with a century-old locomotive and not some modern machine just off the assembly line with the latest in safety controls and fail-safes. We both knew that this was way more complex and dangerous in so many ways.

Samantha knew where we could get all the scrap coal we needed down by the mine where her father worked. There were always small piles left over after they loaded it onto trucks to be transported to the various foundries, factories, and power plants that purchased tonnage for their operations. Over the course of the next few months, we transferred this scrap coal, little by little, until we had a quantity big enough for our test run.

Water was another resource we would need. And we would need a lot of it. Our historical blueprints showed that the *Tullahoma* could hold almost two thousand gallons of water. That was no small quantity, but thankfully there was a well near the rail car shop. We could take turns pumping by hand until we reached an adequate level—if it still worked.

Priming the pump and squeezing oil from an oil can into every crack and crevice, I slowly started moving the handle back and forth to test it out. Some of the brownest, ugliest water I had ever seen came forth, and it reeked of sulfur and decay. After a couple dozen or more pumps, the water began to turn clearer, and although I wouldn't dare drink it, the water looked sufficient for our purposes. We were quite amazed that the well even worked after all these years. Someone had covered the hand pump with a waterproof canvas bag when the railroad shop shut down, and thankfully that kept the components from rusting completely solid.

Fashioning a rubber hose to the pump and running it a few dozen yards into the shop, we slowly started to fill the boiler. While we all wondered if that water would begin oozing out of the welds in the boiler that we couldn't see, which would then need to be re-welded, much to our surprise it held water tighter than a drum. My father had evidently done a fantastic job restoring the boiler, and if it was any indication of how well the wheels that he had also restored would turn, we would be in great shape. We carefully lubricated all of the gears, pistons, crank rods, and every other moving component so that they would easily glide along in the locomotive's maiden test voyage.

Chapter 30

The three of us agreed on a cool day in early March 1963 to give the locomotive its test run. After all, we still needed to ensure that it would safely roll and that there were no major issues. Our grand plan in June at the centennial was to simply pilot it from the repair shop to the other end of the rail yard in front of our house that looked almost directly down Main Street. Our goal was to bring it back to life and prove that this behemoth could still work—definitely not as a youthful workhorse again; those days were long since passed —but to still operate in a minor capacity as we aimed to prove that this Civil War technology could once again ride the rails.

Showing up after breakfast, the three of us got to work right away, shoving coal in the firebox and filling the boiler halfway with water. Samantha pumped only a couple of hundred gallons of water before she said her arms were on fire, so ever trying to be her hero, I took over and pumped. And pumped. And pumped some more, until my arms trembled from muscle fatigue and screamed for oxygen. But finally, we had enough water in the boiler for a quick operational check. Samantha opened all of the transom windows and doors on the repair shop to ventilate the toxic smoke and steam once we lit the firebox—and to disperse the smoke in as many directions as possible so we wouldn't be giving away our covert mission to anyone who might worry if they spotted a large dark plume of concentrated black smoke.

We estimated it would take at least a couple of hours for the water to heat up to the point of producing enough steam to generate initial power. As we waited for the temperature in the boiler to rise, I would periodically hop into the cab to check the gauges and dials, monitor the temperature rise, and add more coal to the firebox. Mr. Smith continuously read from a plethora of notes and books that scattered throughout the workbench as we ensured we covered every detail. Every time I opened the fire door to shovel in coal, I could feel the immensity of the scorching heat. I couldn't imagine the life of a fireman on a locomotive in the 1800s, consumed with sweat, coal ash, heat, the constant vibration of a rumbling train, and fatigue from the scorching sun for hours on end.

After almost two hours of waiting for the process to take place, with the steam pressure at an adequate level, we were ready for our test run. With his limp, it wasn't easy, but I helped Mr. Smith up onto the deck of the train with me while Samantha stayed below. "Okay, we are going to go forward about 75 feet and then stop and reverse. Are you ready?!" Mr. Smith hollered down to Samantha amid the hiss of hydraulics and steam.

Standing there in her overalls and pigtails, she gave us the "thumbs up" sign that we were all ready to give this a shot. I could scarcely believe that the trial moment we had all worked so hard for was finally here. Mr. Smith told me to slowly release the brake, and with a great anything-but-smooth lurch, we inched forward. We were off! I could hear the metal-on-metal sound of the 4-4-0 wheels as they slowly inched forward over the rails.

"How does everything look down there?" Mr. Smith yelled down to Samantha.

Samantha, maintaining a safe distance from the steam discharge, carefully crouched down to inspect the area underneath. Finding no immediate cause for concern, she gave another thumbs up. As we pulled away from the shop, I could see the familiar sight of my house from my elevated vantage point in the locomotive's cab. My mother was hanging laundry on the line, her back turned toward us, and thankfully, we were out of sight of any curious onlookers on the main road. Slowly setting the brake and reversing our control inputs, we reversed the hulking machine back into the shop.

What an incredible experience for a high school kid and his teacher—to drive a century-old train, even if only for about 75 feet each direction to test its operation. Just to feel all of those wheels freely turn under their own power was a glorious feeling. Our trial was complete, and we were confident that we were nearly prepared for the town centennial.

Samantha gave us a big wave when we were back in the position from which we started as she carefully watched our clearances. We extinguished the fire and allowed the water to slowly cool. I let the others know that in another eight hours, I would return to release the coal from the firebox and water from the boiler into the grated drain below so it could sizzle and fully extinguish.

Hopping from the cab and assisting Mr. Smith carefully down the steep ladder near the rear of the locomotive, the three of us let out a whoop and a holler at our excitement that everything had gone surprisingly well. Hugs and high-fives abounded for everyone in joyous celebration. Mr. Smith had brought his 35mm camera along that day and had Samantha and me stand next to the locomotive. He snapped our photo as we were hugging each other in our bulky gray coveralls. Afterwards, he took a few more pictures from different angles of the train.

The day was exciting and fantastic, but the true reward for me was honoring the legacy of a father I never knew. Realizing the goal he had set out to accomplish before being sent off to war filled my heart with a priceless joy. I imagined him smiling down from above, proud of what the three of us —along with his earlier efforts—had all achieved together.

Chapter 31

Later that evening after dinner, I walked back over to the repair shop and climbed up onto the cab. Observing that the water temperature in the boiler had dropped below one hundred and forty degrees, I used a big pipe wrench to turn the washout plugs, and the water came pouring out into the drain grate below. Simultaneously, I released the coal ashes and embers, and the two combined in the trough in a great hiss of steam. We had learned that coal burns extremely hot and is a bit of a challenge to extinguish, but with hundreds of gallons of water released from the boiler at the same time, I was confident that the two elements rendered the hot coals in the drain trough inert.

Stepping into the office while I was waiting for the water to completely drain and the sizzling coal embers to subside, I drafted some ideas and plans to show Mr. Smith and Samantha of how I thought we should decorate the locomotive for the big day ahead. I had saved up a little more of my side job and paper route money, and I thought it would be majestic to adorn the locomotive with American flags and some red, white, and blue bunting.

Of course, the *Tullahoma* was a southern workhorse and predominantly rode the rails in former Confederate territory, from Alabama to Tennessee, Louisiana, Mississippi, Georgia, and beyond. And it was true, a Union ambush had killed the southern crew on this train and damaged the locomotive so badly that it met its demise. But that was a century ago. The nation had coalesced and healed, and time marched on.

Despite many Southern sympathizers and even occasional stories of the KKK running around in the Deep South, I thought we should only fly the American flag. I'd run the thought by Samantha and Mr. Smith but was sure they'd likely agree. Besides, Hawaii had just become the fiftieth U. S. state a few years prior. How amazing would it be to have the new American fifty-star flag adorn this American treasure along with patriotic bunting, bridging the past with the future?

Piercing my thoughts, I heard one of the big machine shop doors open. My mother hollered out for me, "Hey, are you in here?"

It was only one of a handful of times she ever came over to the repair shop; it just wasn't her thing, so I knew she must have something important to relay. I stepped out of the shop's office to greet her as I noticed the last of the water draining out of the locomotive.

"Over here," I yelled. "We gave the train a test run earlier, just a few feet, but it worked beautifully!" I told her.

"Well, just be careful," she said, always the proverbial motherly response to any situation or activity in which I was involved.

Which I always echoed with my regular snarky reply— "Never. I walk on the wild side!"

"I'm glad Mr. Smith has been keeping an eye on you guys," she replied, always the worrier that I'd press things a little too far and get hurt.

To be fair, as the adult, Mr. Smith was diligently overseeing the shop activities, and I deeply valued his expertise and guidance. However, I preferred to think more of the dynamic where I assumed responsibility for Samantha's safety. As the gentleman in the relationship, I counted it my duty to be chivalrous and protective in all our endeavors.

I asked my mother what was up since I was still startled that she had even come over to the shop. Something important must have come up. As she came closer, in her hands was a letter that she handed to me.

"It came in the mail today, and I just saw it and figured you'd want to open it as soon as possible," she said.

Taking the certified letter from her reach, I saw the postmark of "Nashville, Tennessee" at first, and then quickly noticed it was from Belmont. I tore into the envelope quickly —but carefully—and rapidly scanned the letter for those three magic words, the only ones that mattered.

"You've been accepted!" it read.

I hollered out in excitement, my voice echoing throughout the shop so loud that the reverberation echoed off the metal in the shop.

She gave me a huge hug. "I'm proud of you. Hopefully, Samantha got an acceptance letter, too, and you guys can start college together in the fall."

"Can I go call her?" I asked.

"Of course!" Mom replied. So I quickly shut the door to the shop and we hustled back over to the house.

As we walked inside, the phone was ringing. I rolled my eyes as I quickly picked up the receiver, expecting to be annoyed by whomever was tying up the line that I needed in order to call my girlfriend with my oh-so-important news.

"Hello?" I said irritably.

"It's me!" the familiar voice on the other end exclaimed.

It was Samantha. She was calling to tell me *her* great news. She had received an acceptance letter, too, and I told her my exciting news as well. It was official; the two of us would be attending college together in the fall. I was ecstatic that everything seemed to be falling into place. Success with the locomotive test as well as our acceptance letters made it a memorable day for certain.

Chapter 32

In April, still riding a wave of excitement as we neared completion of the locomotive restoration and received our college acceptance letters to Belmont, I finally decided that now was the time to get serious and ask my beloved Samantha to marry me. I made an appointment with Pastor Robert one Saturday morning and met him at the church. Meeting one-on-one was initially somewhat daunting, as my ventures to the church had primarily been limited to Sunday morning services. I must confess that my biblical knowledge, while sincere, did not compare to the academic rigor in which I excelled during my senior year of high school.

"Don't worry," the pastor assured me. "I'm not here to test your biblical knowledge or see what Bible verses you have memorized."

Which was a relief, because in my heightened state of anxiety, I could only recall John 3:16 and some Old Testament lines about "Don't kill," and "Remember the Sabbath and keep it holy." In my nervousness, I couldn't have cited any verses for the life of me if I were asked. *I probably need to start reading my Bible a little more*, I thought to myself in a sobering moment of self-awareness.

During the course of the meeting, Pastor Robert hit on quite a few heavy topics for a high school guy to digest. Nevertheless, he said we needed to talk through them if I was considering a marriage proposal in order for me to be prepared, so we tackled each head-on:

"How would you characterize your personal relationship with God?" he asked.

"Well, I attend church every Sunday, and we pray at home before every meal. Did I read my Bible as much as I should? Not exactly, but it would be something I would be more committed to going forward," I responded.

"In what ways would you be a faithful leader in your home?" was his next question.

"I would strongly encourage Samantha to cultivate a consistent personal prayer time every day for herself," I answered. "I believe it is essential that we both engage in a shared Bible study as frequently as possible. I envision a future where our love for each other would be interwoven and strengthened with a deepening love for God."

Reflecting on our journey, I remembered extending Samantha an invitation to church when she first arrived in town, an invitation she graciously accepted. Witnessing her commitment to her faith had been a source of constant inspiration, and I have found my own spiritual walk strengthened by her own example of commitment.

"How do you and Samantha handle conflict and disagreements?" he asked.

Taking a moment to think to myself, I answered, "We get along pretty well, and we are both very supportive of open discussion. I suppose we'd handle them just as well as any couple would. I know when to engage and when to back away and give her some space."

Hopefully that was the answer the Pastor was looking for, I thought. *Eek!* Nobody likes talking about conflict.

"Have you discussed your plans for children and how you would raise them?" he asked inquisitively.

This question was easy. "We have; we would both like to have two kids. Our ideal vision for the future is for me to obtain a fulfilling career that would provide sufficient financial stability for our family. We hope this will allow Samantha the opportunity to free herself from corporate work in order to spend more time at home with the children, providing them with a nurturing and loving home environment. We envision a future where she would have the flexibility to return to the workforce when our children reached school age, pursuing any professional goals of hers following our children's early daycare years," I responded.

"What are your financial goals for your future family?" he asked.

"To live a comfortable life as a close-knit family unit for better or for worse. Would it be here in Paxton, or would life take us elsewhere? It's too hard to say at our young age, but we would be committed together in our union no matter what, wherever we ended up. I grew up with a single mother who worked as a waitress at the diner, and money was always tight for us, so I was used to living frugally most of my life. Our goal is that, no matter life's circumstances, Samantha and I would be together through thick and thin. As long as we had each other, everything else would shake out in the end," I answered. Pastor Robert nodded in acceptable agreement with my thoughts.

His next question was one of the hardest: "What are your hopes and dreams for the future?"

This was the question that plagued most of my high school career. I was more excited about my long-term future and what I wanted than about the immediacy of going to college or straight into the workforce. "Our near-term goals were to each earn our degrees, although I have yet to figure out how to pay for it," I answered him.

Pastor Robert was excited to hear that we both received acceptance letters to the same university.

"I'd love to shake the dust of this two-horse town off my shoes and move to a bigger city like Huntsville or Nashville. But my dreams are just to support my beau—and our family, if God is gracious enough to bless us with children— wherever that might be."

Pastor Robert mostly sat and listened and nodded quite a bit with my responses. He really didn't say too much. I think he was happy with my replies, though. He had certainly gotten to know my character over the past seventeen years of my life—and Samantha too, over the past year and a half that I had been faithfully bringing her to church with me. Hopefully my support and encouragement of Samantha becoming baptized last year would reflect positively on his favorability of our union.

With his sincerest blessing, Pastor Robert wished us well and said if Samantha accepted my engagement proposal, he would be more than happy to officiate our wedding at the church. With that, he bid me adieu. I felt a great sense of relief that I had made it through that counseling as I pondered all that we had talked about, optimistic about the future.

Chapter 33

A few days later, Mr. Jensen invited me to go to the gun range to shoot trap and skeet with him. I knew that he was a casual quail hunter, and I suppose you can't become an expert Northern Bobwhite marksman without a little practice in the off-season. My mother showed me where my father's old Remington 870 twelve-gauge shotgun was stored in the broom closet of our house, and I found some gun oil with which to clean and lubricate it to ensure it worked flawlessly. I had only handled a shotgun a few times before, so I definitely could use the practice. Eager to prove to the father of the girl I loved that I was a "real man" and willing and able to hang with her father, I figured this would be a great opportunity to bond. Tying the soft-sided gun case to the side of my bike and heading just outside of town, I met Mr. Jensen down by the edge of the city dump.

The dump was sort of an interesting place, and in those days people would throw all of their garbage in a small pass between two ravines. Periodically, a local farmer would push some dirt over the garbage to keep the coyotes and other scavengers from digging into it. The trail leading up to the dump consisted of two deep ruts, and along the left side was a barbed wire fence with a cattle pasture on the other side. On top of every fence post along the lane leading up to the dump, someone had placed either a tire or an old upside-down cowboy boot on top. I never did understand why country folk did that, but the artistic flair gave the lane some fun character.

I'd sometimes venture up there with my .22 rifle, eager to explore the new targets that awaited. Tin cans, old console televisions, and record players were all fair game. But pop bottles, pickle jars, and telegraph pole insulator caps were my targets of choice as their shattered glass provided a satisfying explosion upon breaking. While the minefield of garbage made for a rifle or pistol shooter's delight, it also made a great place over which to shoot clay pigeons with shotguns because of its remoteness.

When I arrived, Mr. Jensen was unloading his clay pigeon launcher from the trunk of his car. Closing his car trunk lid, we laid our gun cases out on top of the makeshift table that the trunk created. He admired my gun, and I handed it to him to examine as he worked the pump action back and forth several times. I told him it was my dad's, and I think he appreciated that I had taken special care to oil and shine it. Sort of a respect and honor among men, I suppose. His gun was an expensive Turkish model, and I admired the intricate metallurgical stenciling that was handcrafted into the side of it, flanked by beautiful dark-stained walnut wood.

We each shot two rounds of clay pigeons, although I only hit about half of the targets in my first round. Getting adjusted to the gun and taking pointers from Mr. Jensen along the way, I was able to increase my accuracy to almost seventy-five percent in the second round. I think Mr. Jensen appreciated having another guy to shoot with since he was raising two daughters, neither of whom had any interest in shotgun shooting. And I appreciated the opportunity to participate in a sport considered skillful and masculine with a man I respected, since the only other particular male role model in my life was Mr. Smith.

Following our enjoyable double round of shooting, laughs, and chatting a bit between throws, I just blurted out: "Mr. Jensen, I really like your daughter Samantha and have fallen in love with her. I'd like to ask for your permission to marry her if I could please have your blessing."

Wow, I can't believe I said that without stammering and stuttering. I spoke as if I had mentally rehearsed it, although in truth, my thoughts were still more of a complexity of jumbled ideas in my mind, and I had still been wondering to myself up until this point when an appropriate time would be to ask him for Samantha's hand in marriage. It definitely wasn't a thought I had formulated prior to an expertly choreographed and rehearsed dance, though.

He looked straight ahead for a minute, a side smirk showing ever so slightly through his pursed lips as he towered above me. I instantly regretted that maybe this wasn't the right moment to ask him. Although it was just the two of us, perhaps a different setting away from guns would have been a safer bet. *Eek!* But then I also thought that, heck, if two men can share in an enjoyable and fun male activity like clay target shooting, then hopefully I had earned a little respect in the maturity bank for having a candid adult conversation. After all, this was me *the young man* asking, and not me the *12th-grade high school kid.*

"All right. . ." he began, slightly turning his six-foot-five muscular frame toward me, though his gaze seemed to avoid direct eye contact. I sensed a degree of emotional tension in his body language, suggesting that this conversation was as challenging for him to continue as it was for me to initiate.

"I was wondering when this moment would come. As long as you promise to always love her and take care of her, then I give you my blessing. But don't feel as though you have to ask her right away. Give it a few more weeks, if you would, at least until the two of you have graduated. But I'd be honored to have you as a son-in-law," he said.

If the heat of that late spring Alabama afternoon hadn't already made my face turn red, I knew I was instantly flushed as the immensity of a tremendous weight lifted from my shoulders in that moment. My chest felt as though I hadn't taken a breath in the past three minutes, and I inhaled and exhaled quickly to get some oxygen into my bloodstream.

"Thank you so much, sir," I said. "Your blessing means so much to me. And thank you for taking me shooting with you this afternoon. I really learned a lot, and I hope we can do it again soon."

"Me too," he said and smiled as he put the last of his unspent shotgun shells in his gun case and zipped up the bag.

Biking home, I felt a surge of euphoria. It was as if I were soaring above the town, two wheels riding on cloud nine. The weight of uncertainty was lifted, replaced by a profound gratitude and excitement. Mr. Jensen's blessing of allowing me to propose to Samantha was a humbling honor.

I hadn't realized it until this moment, but I discovered that there was actually a secret thrill in this waiting period—the anticipatory time in between receiving Mr. Jensen's approval and the moment when I would actually pop the question to Samantha. Gaining his endorsement made me feel like a grown-up, entrusted with a weighty secret. Only Mr. Jensen and I knew of this momentous decision of mine, and his ensuant blessing. I resolved to cherish it, guarding the weighty blessing until the perfect moment. And I would honor Mr. Jensen's request for a brief delay, even though my heart was bursting with the anticipation of popping the question to Samantha.

Chapter 34

Graduation day finally arrived, and I was thrilled yet humbled to be named valedictorian of our class. Eighteen other seniors, including the unlikely duo of Boone and Oliver, had also made it to this milestone. As we crossed the stage, the principal asked each of us to share our future plans with the audience.

Boone and Oliver announced their intention to continue working on the cotton plantation. Samantha and I revealed our plans to attend Belmont University. Other classmates expressed their aspirations to work in the coal mine, labor as farmers, study at the University of Alabama, or pursue trade apprenticeships.

My valedictorian speech deviated from the typical fare. Instead of focusing on individual achievements, I emphasized our shared identity as citizens of Paxton, Alabama, the Class of 1963. Regardless of our gender, race, or socioeconomic status, we were all part of this community. Wherever our paths led, we would carry a piece of Paxton and its foundational experiences with us.

"Life, my friends, is a journey of constant growth, much like the very tobacco and cotton crops that sustain our land and fuel life in our community. Some of us flourish with vibrant ease, while others may find their path more arduous and withering. There will be seasons of abundant growth, and times when progress seems to languish, when doubt whispers that you may wither and never reach your full potential and make it to harvest. Yet, remember this: as Alabamians and as

Americans, we are bound by a shared spirit of resilience as we strive with advancement toward our goals. We are a people who believe in the power of perseverance, who understand that even in the face of adversity, the human spirit can bloom."

As I concluded with a call for unity and hope in the future, the audience erupted in applause. I was overjoyed to see my mother, brother, and his family beaming with pride in the crowd as they applauded.

Following graduation, tables and chairs were set up on the front lawn of the school, and there was a huge luncheon for all of the graduates and visitors. I warmly greeted Samantha with a brief hug and offered my congratulations, but then excused myself, allowing her to fully enjoy the company of her family, including extended relatives who had traveled all the way from Pennsylvania. Mr. Smith came up to congratulate me and shake my hand, and my mother quickly invited him to join us at our table for lunch, where we had as much delicious picnic food and lemonade as our stomachs could handle.

After the luncheon, as the crowds started to disperse, I stepped over to the side of the lawn as I took one last look back at the school in a quiet moment of reflection. It was a place where so many personal life transformations had taken place. A place that I would likely never have a reason to step into again.

It's a juxtaposition of sorts, how a place can be so lively, filled with people, noise, energy, and emotion one moment—like on this graduation day—but then fall as silent and still as the new fallen snow on a dark winter's night. Just as the locomotive, once powerful and roaring with life, now sits silent in the repair shop awaiting its next journey and a second life. The contrast between former energy and current stillness is a stark reminder of the impermanence of life.

Mr. Smith's presence unexpectedly interrupted the train of thought in which I was currently engaged.

"Sorry you weren't successful in getting any of those scholarships you applied for. I just heard the news from your mother," he told me. "Keep trying; there's lots of time between now and when college starts. There's always a chance something else might break later this summer; you never know."

I expressed thanks for his cordiality and said at least I thought I'd be able to attend one year at Belmont—even if that was all I could afford before possibly dropping out before my second year due to lack of funds.

Sensing stress and apprehension in my body language and quickly changing the subject to liven my mood, Mr. Smith said, "Well, we can get started on the last-minute locomotive preps next week if you want." I nodded and said that I'd meet him in a few days. Samantha's relatives would be heading home the following week, and then our team effort would reconvene following the excitement of graduation to put the finishing touches on our restoration project.

Chapter 35

The town's centennial was rapidly approaching. Our immediate task involved clearing the overgrown weeds that had encroached upon the railway spur connecting the repair shop to the main line. This spur bisected our property and ran parallel to the main road, affording curious onlookers a clear view of our efforts.

As we wielded scythes and shovels, clearing the tracks of vegetation, passing vehicles would occasionally honk. I'm sure we appeared as an unsightly chain gang of sorts as we labored. Thankfully, the task was not as daunting as it initially appeared. Within a few hours, we had cleared a sufficient length of track. Fortuitously, the track switch was in the correct position, and the rails appeared to be in decent shape despite their age, still retaining thick clay and white rocks to solidly ensconce them as if embedded in concrete.

We carefully checked our coal supply to ensure a quantity such that the engine could be moved just far enough into a prominent position for the town to see. Patriotic decorations that Samantha expertly hung—buntings, flags, and streamers—transformed the locomotive into a festive spectacle, fit for a presidential whistle-stop tour.

The three of us took final stock of our objectives for the day, and our plan was to arrive early on the morning of the centennial to fill the boiler and heat the water. We all grew excited at the notion that the entire town would be awestruck as the *Tullahoma*—an antique archaeological phoenix rising from the ashes—chugged into full view at the end of the town's centennial parade route.

The next morning, on the day of the celebration, I awoke at 6:00 a.m. so that I could complete my paper route as early as possible. I wanted to get to the shop by 7:30 a.m. to start filling the boiler with water. Nearly every business in town would be closed for the celebration, plus we were expecting an influx of at least a thousand people from nearby towns. It was exactly 100 years ago to the day that Paxton was founded, and almost 100 years ago that the Union raid disabled the *Tullahoma*—essentially sending it underground and forgotten for the next century—so how fitting that we planned to reveal it exactly a century later. Peering down Main Street at the early hour, it was largely quiet except for a few cars that I could see parked outside the Redbird Cafe for the few morning hours that it was open for breakfast, before it would be closed the rest of the day for the centennial.

As I lit a fire in the firebox, Samantha and Mr. Smith walked in around the same time, both as excited as I was. It was now a waiting game for the coal to heat the water so that the locomotive would be ready to move under its own power on schedule mid-morning, to be in position at the junction at the end of the street where the parade ended.

"Well, guys, this is it! Thank you so much for all of your hard work; it's been so much fun to rescue this engine and bring it back to life as a team," I told the others as we waited for the boiler to heat. "I don't know what will happen after today. I suppose we will just pull her back into the shop here again, but at least we did our part in saving a piece of our history. Perhaps it can end up in a museum someday."

Soon enough, Samantha and I would be off to college, and our high school journey of rescuing this historical artifact would be history itself. But for now, we just wanted to enjoy our special moment in this place and time. As I climbed into the locomotive cab to operate the engine, I offered Mr. Smith a hand up to join me.

"No, you kids do it," he said, beaming with excitement. "It's all yours. Have fun, and I'll walk alongside."

I couldn't help but protest. "Are you sure? You've been so important to this project in reaching this point. Your knowledge and expertise have been so gracious and valuable in getting us this far."

He waved me off again, and I reluctantly nodded. But even as I released the brake lever, I couldn't shake the feeling that he belonged up in the engineer's cab with Samantha and me.

Slowly pulling out of the shop, steadily but surely, the sun shone on the engine to reveal its shiny appearance as it glinted in the sun, the light of day reflecting off the freshly painted metal as if coming off the assembly line for the first time. I felt powerful and strong as I commanded the behemoth forward, as we had during testing a few weeks prior. This time, Samantha was alongside me as my co-engineer.

Just as the engine was beginning to exit the shop, we heard a loud *Bang!* Fearing something catastrophic with the fire versus steam ratios that we were always trying to carefully balance, I instantly glanced at the gauges, and everything appeared to be within operating limits. No red lines had been exceeded, although we seemed to be losing steam pressure rapidly. Samantha looked out the left side window, and Mr. Smith was waving his arms.

"I think you just blew a cylinder!" he exclaimed. "You aren't going anywhere like that. I think we are dead in the water."

I looked at the steam gauges again and could see the pressure was now way below the normal range and rapidly dropping. During our months of study, I remembered reading that cylinders on these old engines sometimes blew, often due to issues like a faulty valve, a broken piston ring, or a lack of lubrication, causing the cylinder to rupture. As I craned my neck outside the front of the cab to peer forward, I could see massive amounts of hydraulic fluid and water gushing onto the wooden railroad ties and white rock below.

Oh, please no! I thought, after a year and a half of hard work, massive amounts of prepping, and the emotional high of being able to show off our project to the town on this special occasion. *There's no way this moment could be over that quick—before it even happened, really.* I set the brake and hopped down to look, my boots landing in the middle of water and muck. Metal fragments and shards sat soaked in black oil as the smell of hot lubricant filled the air. We most certainly couldn't operate the train like that. Halfway out of the barn, we were completely disabled. Our locomotive journey had hit the proverbial end of the line.

In the far distance, we could hear the school band starting to warm up. The parade was soon to start, and we had less than an hour before the fête was over. We would now likely never get to show off our passion project that we had resurrected. I suppose if we had a bulldozer, we could tug it the short distance we needed, but none of us knew of any piece of machinery big enough that could be arranged in time. Samantha didn't think a tractor from the mine could be brought up here that quickly—should her dad even have permitted it—and a machine operator on hand who could have driven it.

Just then, a light bulb went off in my head. It was as if the Lord Himself had intervened, providing a clear pathway forward.

Though unsure of its success, I shouted to Mr. Smith, "Help Samantha with the temperature gauges and shut everything down! I have a plan—it's a long shot, but it's our best bet. I need at least thirty minutes, though."

Without even giving them time to object or ask questions, I raced out of the shop, not knowing if I would be successful or not, but charged with the virtue of at least trying and giving it my best attempt. I ran over to the house, jumped on my bike, and pedaled as fast as I could west of town, feeling the momentum of adrenaline carry me, but also the feeling as if I were heading into a blackening western stormy sky. I knew I'd probably be walking into a powder keg, but it was worth a shot after all the hard work we had done so far.

Chapter 36

Arriving at the shanty of Boone and Oliver, I started hollering for them before I even jumped off and dropped my bike, fearing they'd hear someone quickly coming up their rock road and bear shotguns in defense. I was certain that these two imbeciles would not be caught dead downtown at something as fun and lively as a parade, so they would most likely be hanging near home. Seeing the smoke from a small campfire surrounded by rocks, I could tell someone was there as I dropped my bike. Rife with fear, I walked up the daunting Valley of Gehenna to their ramshackle house.

A hulking Doberman that was chained near the cabin's edge must have startled awake when it heard me dismount from my bike. It jumped up and lunged, baring and gnashing its teeth. Thankfully, the heavy chain it was tied to held firm, but the commotion instantly drew the attention of the Tybalt brothers, who whirled around to find me approaching.

"What in the hell are you doing here, what do you want?!" They hollered at me as they stood up from a couple of stumps cut into stools that surrounded a fire pit. A rudimentary cast iron assembly was positioned over the flame for cooking and it looked like they had just finished eating breakfast. "And why in the hell are you wearing overalls so filthy that you look like you've been rolling around in a coal pit?"

I explained to them the CliffsNotes version of the locomotive that we had restored, and how we planned to drive it a few hundred yards to be the focal point at the end of the parade route. The locomotive was the exact one that Mr. Smith had recalled in the story to our history class the school year prior. They were in complete disbelief that we had driven this locomotive a few feet once before, since they only knew me as the nerdy valedictorian from high school and not some sort of mechanical whiz adept in heavy machinery operation.

"Listen," I said. "We blew a piston and can't move the train under its own power. But the wheels still turn fine."

I explained that I had seen a photo in a book once where a locomotive in Raquette Lake, New York, ran out of water two miles from town and couldn't make it to the next station, so they hitched horses to pull it the last two miles. In the early days of trolleys, I also knew that horses were used to pull trolley cars full of people. In our case, we just needed to go a couple hundred yards, and I had confidence that we could tap that same horsepower.

"You guys have a team of mules, and I have seen you out working in the fields and know you both are excellent mule drivers," I said as I boosted their egos with a little bit of puffed praise. "Would you please help us out?" I pleaded with them.

Boone didn't say anything. With tobacco tucked under his lip, he spit to the side as he mulled it over. I could see Oliver drawing circles in the ashes of the campfire with a stick, looking away like he was on the fence at the notion but was at least was entertaining the idea. They were straddling the line, and I needed to find a way to seal the deal.

"Boone, remember last year when I came upon your truck bent around that tree? I was the one who pulled you out and went and got help," I stated.

"Yeah, but then when the sheriff brought me home, my daddy whipped me for wrecking the truck," he replied.

"I'm sorry," I said. "But when you didn't come home with the truck one way or the other, he was going to find out about it anyhow, wasn't he? At least I took time to stop that night to make sure you were okay."

That emotional appeal didn't exactly help my plight as much as I thought it would. Oliver continued drawing in the campfire ashes with his head tilted downward, not saying anything as he listened on.

I will have to pull out the nuclear arsenal, I thought to myself. *Here goes nothing.*

Speaking softly, since I didn't know if their daddy was within earshot, I said to them, "I know that it was you guys who burned down the mill."

For the first time in our conversation, Oliver stopped tracing circles in the dirt below his feet and looked up. "Bull crap!" he said. "Everybody in town is blaming us, I know, but it's just because of our reputation. Not because they actually have any evidence or saw us or anything."

I went on to tell them I was there, and so was Samantha. They both just stared at me dumbfounded, as if they were conducting a mental "fight or flight" action in response, mulling it over, not knowing exactly the extent of what I actually claimed to know. As I went on, I explained that we were sitting out on the waterwheel when we heard their dirt bikes roll up. I told them exactly where they were standing, that it was their second joint inside the mill when the lit cigarette was dropped, at which point they jumped back on their bikes and left. I told them that Samantha and I had to jump into the creek to save ourselves and swim to safety because we were trapped by the flames and it was our only path of escape.

By this time, I knew they could tell I wasn't bluffing—they recognized from the details that we were truly there.

"But here's the thing," I said. "I never ratted you guys out once and don't plan to. Never even confronted you guys about it. Neither did Samantha. We are willing to take that secret to the grave. All I'm asking is, will you please help us out just this once? This is your chance for redemption, to do something good for this community. You both graduated, same as I did. I know you'll be working on the plantation here come fall; that's what you both said at graduation. You'll be sticking around this town and all of the people in it. This is your chance to do something positive—to lend a hand and do something nice that this town will remember you for. And I promise you, from now until the grave, I won't tell anyone about the old mill you caught on fire. And neither will Samantha."

They both looked at each other, as if their eyes were telepathically having a conversation and discussing it between each other. They both then reluctantly agreed to help out. *Yes! Those interpersonal communication and conflict resolution courses I took in ninth grade finally paid off!* I thought to myself.

I thanked them immensely as we hastened to push a wagon over next to Belteshazzar, Hananiah, Mishael, and

Azariah, their four mules. As the mules sauntered over from the far side of the corral, letting out brays in protest while coming forth, I then helped to harness them up. By now, I figured that Mr. Smith and Samantha thought I had died, but hopefully, they hadn't completely given up hope.

I threw my bike in the back of the wagon, and we were soon off, rumbling down the highway at a brisk pace, as if we were stuck somewhere between a 1950s western and runaway Amish lads on rumspringa. Luckily, with all of the townspeople at the parade and celebration in town, nobody was out driving on this particular Saturday morning, and no cars passed us as we made our way back to the repair shop.

On our way, as Oliver kept a swift pace on the team of mules, Boone apologized for being a jerk and said he was just sick of this town and that it made him bitter and cold. I understood his frustration with Paxton's limited opportunities. It was undeniably a far cry from vibrant and electric big-city life. However, he told me that his anger stemmed primarily from his father's struggles with financial hardship, alcohol, and a lack of upward mobility, perpetuating their cycle of disadvantage. He confided in me that he had decided to enlist in the Army later that year, to which I congratulated him on his decision to join the military. I thanked him for his apology, too. While the Army would be mentally tough, I offered him encouragement as I reminded him that as a star football player, he should have no trouble handling the physical rigors of boot camp.

Chapter 37

As we pulled into the rail yard, Samantha was sitting on the front of the locomotive just above the cowcatcher, her knees pulled up. She slid down the slick red rails when she saw us rolling up, a trail of dust in our wake. Mr. Smith was up top in the cab but poked his head out and climbed down when he saw us coming. Boone and Oliver said their quick hellos as they looked at the locomotive in disbelief, and we quickly unhitched the team from the wagon and positioned them in front of the locomotive as I relayed my harebrained plan to the others of having the mules tug the engine the couple of hundred yards that we needed.

As I ran inside the shop to find a thick rope that would be large enough to connect the mule harness to the locomotive engine, we could hear the sound of the band get steadily louder as they approached the north end of Main Street. They were the final parade act before the fire truck closed out the rear. We had to act quickly.

Samantha and I scurried up to the cab and released the brake, and we could see the mules strain against the weight of the engine. *I know this should work; I've seen it work in a history book,* I thought to myself as I tried to mentally gauge how many gallons of water might be left in the boiler and the weight of the engine the mules were straining to pull. It would just be a matter of getting the initial momentum and inertia started. . . At least, I hoped.

Slowly, after several agonizing moments of the mules straining against the weight of the great iron engine as Boone and Oliver yipped and yelled at them to giddy up, the great locomotive began to creep forward. We were slowly rolling at last. We made our way around the bend in the rails to the main track and our intended position just beyond the top of Main Street. While it wasn't nearly as ideal as we had envisioned being able to do it under our own locomotive power, we found a way to make it work.

Such is life, I suppose.

The sleek black locomotive with its red striping and white lettering glistened in the late morning sun. I hoped that while we weren't able to drive this locomotive into position under its own power, perhaps someday it could be repaired and a more thorough restoration completed.

From our perch in the cab, still unnoticed by the townsfolk, we could see the signature fire truck bringing up the rear of the parade as people at the beginning of the parade route were now starting to disperse. Samantha reached up, and with one long and one short blast of the whistle from the residual steam still left in the pipes, everybody halted their exit and all faces turned in our direction. The mules jumped from the startle of the whistle, and Oliver shot us a scowl from below.

"Better not do that again," I laughed to Samantha. "But nice job on polishing up that whistle! It looks sharp up there against the sleek black pufferbelly."

Reaching up near the ceiling of the locomotive cab, she yanked the bell cord, its resonant clang echoing through the morning air as though the Liberty Bell proclamation of freedom. The piercing sound evoked the spirit of the open rails, a nostalgic echo of the locomotive's triumphant past as it once traversed the vast expanse and freedom of the rails.

We could now see kids running over in our direction with flags and streamers from the parade still in hand, followed by their parents and other old-timers who could perhaps recall the era of trains running on these very tracks—albeit two decades prior. When we were at the apex of being directly at the end of Main Street where it creates a "T," I set the brake and told Boone and Oliver we had reached our mark. I could see Mr. Smith tell the brothers they were clear to unhitch the team of mules and free to go.

A wave of disbelief washed over the onlookers as they approached in droves, pointing toward the restored Civil War era engine. The crowd continued to grow even larger, drawn by the spectacle of this shiny black engine that from their vantage seemed to appear out of nowhere. Even participants in the parade—band members, veterans in their sharply pressed uniforms, and an equestrian team—were captivated, marveling at the unexpected sight. Samantha and I waved back excitedly, and we saw several flashbulbs from a newspaper reporter who likely thought he was headed home after the parade, yet stumbled onto an incredible exclusive story that his editor certainly wouldn't be expecting.

We had accomplished our ultimate goal—positioning the locomotive at the top of Main Street, ready for its centennial unveiling to the town—albeit not exactly how we envisioned it due to the piston failure that disabled the engine. From the engineer's seat, I watched the Tybalt brothers and their mules drive off toward their plantation.

Despite our setback, we had succeeded against all odds. It reinforced a growing understanding in my young life that I was now beginning to realize: God often answers prayers in unexpected ways. He did so in my chance meeting with Samantha. And in the way my mom always managed to feed our family and make ends meet. He provided a deep spot in the river for Samantha's baptism when she gave her life to Jesus, and another deep spot that saved both of our lives when we had to jump to escape the burning mill. He even provided a connection to the father I never met but yearned to know through the restoration of this historic locomotive—a project my father began and a legacy I would then fulfill. Soon, I would witness one more miracle, one that would once again profoundly shape my life. God wasn't done quite yet.

Amid the commotion, Mr. Smith hollered for Samantha and me to step down from the cab, and he told us that there was someone he wanted us to meet. A distinguished-looking gentleman wearing a trilby was standing next to him.

"Hey guys, this is Mr. Harrison Bailey from the National Geographic Society," Mr. Smith's introduction began. "Remember back in March when we did that test run of the engine and I had my camera with me? I snapped several photographs and sent them away to the National Geographic Society, along with a nomination for the Hubbard Award that the Society gives every year for distinction in exploration, discovery, and research. They were so enthralled with our work that you guys won! I've been keeping it a secret for a couple of weeks now."

Samantha and I were speechless. Mr. Bailey held out his hand and placed a gold medallion in each of our palms. The newspaper reporter who had noticed the moment snapped a photo of us as we each marveled at the beautiful gold coins we were handed.

"Not only that," Mr. Bailey added, "But we are awarding a $50,000 prize to be split between the two of you. I understand you were each accepted to Belmont College in Nashville this fall. That's fantastic, and congrats to you both! This money will go pretty far in paying your tuition if you wish to use it for college. And we'd also love to have you give a presentation in Washington, D. C. later this summer about your incredible locomotive discovery and restoration efforts before you both head off for college. Here's my business card; give me a call in a couple of days and we'll arrange your travel expenses to fly you to Washington and present your certificates to you in a more formal ceremony.

I'm sure the Smithsonian Institution and other museums will be reaching out soon enough and will be highly interested in you donating or selling this locomotive to be placed in a museum. I would love it if you do, but between you and me, I also think it would be kind of nice if it stayed right here in Paxton and could be a showpiece for your town. Lots of important connections right here, and it's always nice keeping a piece of history right where it took place instead of in a faraway museum." With that, he tipped his hat to us and faded off into the crowd to examine the engine in more detail.

Tears running down my cheek from the overwhelming emotional ride, I picked Samantha up and spun her around. We pulled each other in tight for a great big bear hug, and I kissed her. "We did it," I smiled, my voice hoarse from the dryness that comes after hard work, hot weather, and an intense adrenaline rush. "This will give us a huge financial boost toward our tuition without worrying about how we will pay for college. Especially me, because I knew I didn't have the money to pay for all four years."

I hugged her again, and she hugged me back; I was just too excited to let her go. I knew my father would be smiling down from above, proud of my hard work and dedication to continuing the mission that he had started twenty years prior, as we honored his legacy by bringing this locomotive and its story into the light.

This is the moment, I thought. Dropping to one knee as I crouched near the back of the locomotive in my dirty boots and coveralls, Samantha stood facing the coal tender while other people continued to mill around the machine in amazement.

Clearing my throat as I reached out for her hand and she spun around, I said, "Samantha, from the first time I saw you bounding up the school stairs, I was captivated. Even without knowing your name at that moment, I knew I would fall in love and marry you one day. Over the past year and a half, getting to know you has ignited every spark within me. My love for you grows stronger with each passing day. Whether we're exploring new adventures together or simply enjoying coffee or a soda at the Redbird Cafe, every moment with you is a precious gift. I hope we will have many more magical moments together. Will you please make me your husband?"

As I went to stand up, now it was Samantha who was the one crying as she simultaneously wiped the happy tears from her eyes and brushed the wavy locks back behind her ears. "Yes!" she exclaimed, as she squeezed me in a tight hug.

I reached into my overalls to pull out a black velvet box that contained a ring, which I had placed in my pocket earlier that morning. Taking the ring out of the box, I slipped it onto her ring finger.

Locked in and laser-focused on that moment, I was oblivious to the fact that so many people had gathered around us until they clapped and shouted following Samantha's proclamation of "yes." We both blushed and waved to the crowd, smiling as we kissed and hugged again while they waved their flags and streamers in celebration.

Today was truly one for the books. Off to the side, I spotted my mom and Mr. Smith hugging in celebration as well, overcome by emotion—both from watching Samantha and me grow into adulthood and commit to a future together, but also as they themselves had grown closer in their own burgeoning friendship. Samantha's parents were there, too. The day's excitement and energy overflowed today.

Chapter 38

A few weeks later that same summer, Samantha and I traveled from Birmingham to Washington, D. C., on a TWA 707. The National Geographic Society furnished us with a couple of luxurious rooms at the Willard Hotel, right down the street from the White House, and we were allowed to order any food we wanted from the menu. Each morning, Samantha and I would meet in the lobby for breakfast, and we had some of the best scones, croissants, fresh berries, bacon, and coffee that we had ever tasted while dining at tables with fancy white linen tablecloths.

We crammed as much as we could into our trip—exploring museums, seeing all the nearby monuments, and even meeting our local congressman in his D. C. office. He apologized for missing the unveiling of our newly discovered national treasure but expressed interest in seeing it for himself on a future visit back to his home district. Samantha and I were honored that our achievement had even garnered the attention of a local political dignitary.

Our speech at the National Geographic Society went splendidly, and although I didn't know who any of the hundred or so people were in the audience, I appreciated that we all shared the same love of exploration, discovery, and historical preservation. Samantha interjected a few times, and I was so proud to let her share some specifics regarding the whistle, bell, and headlamp she had personally attended to restoring. Her humor, as she recalled the lighter side of how oily and filthy we would get each day and how we were spooked by a raccoon at the beginning of our adventure, elicited raucous laughs from the crowd. In those moments, I reflected upon our growth together this past year and a half, and I was proud that I would soon be marrying this amazing woman and could finally call her my wife.

I shared with the audience that, after much thought, we planned to keep the *Tullahoma* in Paxton and wanted this slice of American history to remain right in the hometown where its Civil War roots ended and its new future would soon begin—not in some stuffy museum in D. C. or New York or someplace like that. For the time being, the locomotive had a snug spot in the old repair shop building, but we hoped to keep the historical significance of it right where it took place.

Our original hope was that the engine could be restored to fully working condition, but we quickly realized that the decomposition of time had taken its toll on the effective operation of it. Safety and reliability were no longer the possibilities we had hoped for, and we decided that it would be better honored as a display piece. Our revised plan was to eventually have it transported to our city park in Paxton as a monument where kids or adults of any age could climb on it and pretend to "ride the rails" as they dream of adventure and excitement themselves. Although the locomotive might no longer traverse the South, our restoration efforts were not a complete loss by any means and would go far in preparing the train for its next grandeur assignment. Thanking the constituents in attendance for their gracious medallions, certificates, and prize money, we headed to the airport and caught our flight back home.

On the plane ride back, Samantha and I talked of our mutual desire to get married in late August, the next-to-last Saturday of the month. We decided upon a small wedding at the church with close friends and family, a simple potluck in the church fellowship hall, and a quick honeymoon to Gulf Shores before we would have to return and get ready for college that started right after Labor Day. We came up with a list of a few friends to invite, including her grandparents who would once again come in from northern Pennsylvania. Following our wedding and a few fun days at the shore together, we would then need to return home to pack up for college.

As the plane's tires touched down in Birmingham, I squeezed Samantha's hand reassuringly, that all would be okay as long as the two of us had each other by our side.

Chapter 39

Our wedding a few weeks later wasn't extravagant by any stretch of the imagination, but it was perfect for us. I ended up spending $950 of my award money and bought a used 1958 Oldsmobile 88. Car culture permeated the 1960s, and I had always looked forward to having one of my own, but now I truly needed one for practical utilitarian reasons. Although it wasn't the most sought-after automobile on the market by any stretch, it was as shiny and sleek as a rocket ship and had a powerful engine. Plus, it had a roomy trunk in which we could place our luggage when we honeymooned at the shore and later to pack our clothes and other items into once we headed off to college.

The night before our wedding, I could scarcely sleep; I was so excited for the next day. I crawled out of bed early the next morning and decided to go for a walk. Daylight had just begun to creep over the willow tree that flanked the eastern edge of our yard, and I was mesmerized by the dappled light that filtered through the leaves on this windless, calm summer morning. I crossed over the tracks in front of our house, passed the county highway, and took a stroll down Main Street to its southern end. As I strolled south, I passed by the town park and the Redbird Cafe on the way, the only business that was open at this early morning hour. Over in the distance, two blocks to the west, I could see the top of the school and the church that sat beside it.

Walking farther south, I spotted Samantha's house in the distance. The automobiles of her extended relatives in town for our wedding rested in the driveway. A light shone from her bedroom window, so I knew she was probably awake as well. As I crossed over Main Street and walked back to the north, I passed in front of the fire station and could spot the two engines housed inside. A block north of that, my brother's storefront window housed a summer display that advertised paintbrushes and gardening supplies to passersby. Continuing towards home, I passed by the police station and clinic. All of these places were deeply ingrained in the tapestry of my childhood and upbringing, creating vivid memories that would endure long after I departed for college. Upon my return visits home, I knew that they would offer a sense of comforting familiarity, a welcome reminder of my roots.

Before I walked back inside my house, though, I slipped through the rusty metal gate and opened the door to the locomotive repair shop one final time; the vapors of residual coal and stale oil hung heavy in the air within its walls. That now-familiar shop smell had a Proustian effect over me, one that I had come to relish each time I entered. It had the same comforting power as the fragrance of my mother's homemade chocolate chip cookies or pot pie, a familiar aroma that always evoked feelings of home. It was a final chance to reflect on such an important and exciting chapter in my youthful history as I anticipated and prepared for the next one ahead—marriage and the adventure of college.

As I stood there in the stillness of the building, a silent reverence filled me. I offered up a quiet prayer of gratitude, acknowledging the profound legacy my father had left behind and the privilege I had been afforded to contribute to its continuation. The thought of future generations learning about this restored locomotive, a testament to the resilience and enduring spirit of our community, filled me with a profound sense of satisfaction and a quiet hope for its future in what we had accomplished.

The experience of the last two years not only connected me to my father, whom I had yearned to know my entire life, but with the chapter of the *Tullahoma* at a close, it gave me a personal sense of peace and healing as I could fully let go of my longings of wanting to *know* him. This great project offered me that connection I had so desired in countless ways. Now I truly *knew* him and how the spirit of his life reflected the same adventurous passion of my own inner being.

Rescuing this historical locomotive also offered the town of Paxton a pathway to healing as well. The mystery of its whereabouts was solved, and a chapter of the town's Civil War history could conclusively be placed to rest; the iron wheels of time turning ever onward.

As a young man who loved reading and discovery, I was always drawn to the spirit of the "rail riders," those itinerant young men who often hopped freight trains between towns during the Great Depression, seeking opportunity, adventure, and a better life. The term itself, coined some thirty years earlier, resonated deeply within me.

Now, as I stepped over the footbridge from boyhood to manhood, I came to the profound realization that my experiences, particularly those of exploration and adventure, had indelibly shaped my own coming-of-age identity. I am the boy who rode the rails. Not in the literal sense, of course, but rather through a chance discovery and the mysteries this locomotive held. The *Tullahoma* first connected me with my late father, but it later became a symbol of my own yearning for escape. Though I never hopped a literal train, the journey it symbolized charted the course of my youth—including young love that I found along the way—and personal growth that led me to a deeper understanding of myself and the world around me. Now, through a series of fortunate and serendipitous events and a financial windfall, the *Tullahoma* was carrying me further onward to Belmont in Nashville.

As I closed the large metal doors of the shop one final time, my melancholic longings gave me a sense of peace as I looked forward to the excitement that lay before me. With that, I walked back to the house and bounded up the steps to begin preparing for the exciting wedding day ahead.

Chapter 40

Our wedding day was beautiful under a picture-perfect, pastoral sky. The church was ornately adorned with brilliant sunflowers and calla lilies, as chosen by Samantha. Our ceremony was quite small, with only a few close friends and family, but that was just perfect for us. Our own little intimate moment.

Just prior to our ceremony, Samantha and her family drove up in her dad's car, and I walked down the front steps of the church to greet her.

"Wow, you look absolutely amazing, my love!" I told her as I admired her beautiful white gown and reached for her hand to help her out of the car. Samantha blushed in response. Neither of us lent any credence to the silly old superstition of seeing each other before we walked down the aisle.

"I want to borrow you for a second before we go inside though, please?" I said.

She motioned to her mother that she would be along in just a moment. Taking Samantha's hand in mine, I led her down the sidewalk that wrapped around behind the church.

"Where are we going? There's nothing back here?" she said, confused.

"I know, that's why it's perfect. Just the two of us in a moment of privacy today," I replied. "I just wanted to say a prayer together real quick before our wedding."

Reaching for her other hand, and now firmly holding each of hers in each of mine as we were shielded from view by anyone else but ourselves in this rare moment on our wedding day, I closed my eyes.

"Dear God, I give you this marriage on which we are about to embark. Please grant Samantha and me an unshakable bond with each other. Pour out your blessings on us today and forever, and give us peace and patience in all circumstances. We honor you with our marriage as we join together with you, a three-strand cord that cannot be broken when we trust and abide in you. Give us safe travel to the shore as we head for our honeymoon later this afternoon. Oh, and thanks again for blessing me with such a beautiful girl; she is smoking hot! In Jesus' name, we pray, Amen."

I opened my eyes a fraction of a moment before Samantha opened hers, and she giggled at the last part.

"You better get used to it now, because you never know what's going to come out of my mouth," I told her.

"Oh, don't I already know it?" she replied, rolling her dark brown eyes in playful disdain.

As we walked back to the front of the church to enter inside, I handed my brother, who was our usher, a '45 with "Let it Be Me" to be played once we said our "I dos." A song that forever became "our song" after Samantha and I first heard it on the radio while working in the shop months prior.

Among the small crowd at our wedding were two completely unexpected guests: Boone and Oliver. I never thought they'd come, though I never would have particularly thought to invite them anyhow. However, in a small town, it's hard to keep any news such as a wedding a secret, and they could have easily figured out where and when the ceremony was taking place. One side of me gritted my teeth, wishing they didn't stumble in to trample our big day. But then I recalled those words of my father that my mother would often echo that had a way of penetrating my thoughts at peculiar times in my life: "Whenever you feel like criticizing anyone, just remember that all the people in this world haven't had the advantages that you've had." I then warmly smiled in the direction of the last pew in which they sat, and they both nodded back to me. It was clear after so many times that our paths had crossed in recent years; they were imbued in my life as much as I was in theirs, despite us being as alike as chalk and cheese.

It was a poignant reminder that everyone, regardless of their background, has a place in this world. Boone and Oliver, from the other side of the tracks, lived vastly different lives than Samantha and me. Yet, we all intersected within the unique community tapestry here in Paxton, Alabama. Reflecting on our diverse experiences and varying levels of advantages, I realized that we were much like threads in a quilt—a paradox of sorts. Individual threads, like a plate of spaghetti, appear aimless and seemingly awry. But when those various threads are woven together, they create a beautiful and unified masterpiece, collectively forming something quite extraordinary.

And isn't life in general like that? We are largely insignificant on our own but become radiantly beautiful when intertwined in the community we create. Perhaps even a glimpse of what Heaven will one day look like, as beauty is recognized by us and affirmed by God. Redemption strengthens the threads that bind us together despite our complex backgrounds and upbringings, making us more interconnected and interdependent upon each other.

When Samantha walked down the aisle of the church a few minutes later, she looked as pretty and fair as the morning dew, adorned in the purest white dress and kissed by the feminine touches of baby's breath and orange blossoms in her hair. The silver heart necklace I had given to her our first Christmas as a couple adorned her neck. Her father shook my hand as he passed her tender arm from his to mine. We recited our vows beneath the cross that hung at the front of the sanctuary, my six-foot-three-inch frame standing sentinel over the young woman I would swear allegiance to protect and love for the rest of my life.

Happiness surged through me, filling every ventricle and recess of my heart. Looking towards the future, I felt a profound gratitude and appreciation for my past, but I couldn't wait to see where life would take us next. With that, we said our "I dos" and embraced in a long kiss as our family and friends clapped and cheered.

"I love you on purpose," I softly spoke so that only Samantha could hear, eliciting a tight embrace from her in response.

"Let it Be Me" played loudly from a record player at the back of the sanctuary as we exited the church, and our dearest family, friends, and guests clapped and threw rice in celebration. I couldn't wait to discover what life's next great adventure was for us, wherever the Lord might lead us, as we powered forward along the rails of life—full steam ahead.

A Note From The Author

Thank you for reading my book! If you enjoyed it, I'd be incredibly grateful if you could take a moment to leave a review wherever you purchased it.

Reviews are the lifeblood of an author's career. They help new readers discover my work, influence visibility on online platforms, and directly impact my ability to continue writing books like this one. Even a brief, honest review makes an enormous difference.

Your words matter more than you know, and I read every single review with gratitude.

Happy reading,

Brent

www.ingramcontent.com/pod-product-compliance
Lightning Source LLC
Chambersburg PA
CBHW051108030726
47504CB00006B/1843